The Dog Days of Charlotte Hayes

Marlane Kennedy

Greenwillow Books

An Imprint of HarperCollins*Publishers*

The Dog Days of Charlotte Hayes
Copyright © 2009 by Marlane Kennedy

The text of this book is set in Caslon.
Book design by Victoria Jamieson

Library of Congress Cataloging-in-Publication Data

Kennedy, Marlane.
The dog days of Charlotte Hayes / by Marlane Kennedy.
p. cm.
"Greenwillow Books."
Summary: Eleven-year-old Charlotte is not a dog person but does not like that the rest of her family neglects their Saint Bernard puppy, and so with a lot of determination and a little sneakiness, she works on finding a good home for the gentle giant.
ISBN 978-0-06-145241-3 (trade bdg.)
ISBN 978-0-06-145242-0 (lib. bdg.)
[1. Family life—West Virginia—Fiction. 2. Saint Bernard dog—Fiction. 3. Dogs—Fiction. 4. Moneymaking projects—Fiction. 5. Old age—Fiction. 6. Babies—Fiction. 7. West Virginia—Fiction.]
I. Title.
PZ7.K3846Dog 2009   [Fic]—dc22
2008007507

First Edition 10 9 8 7 6 5 4 3 2 1

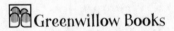 Greenwillow Books

✵ ✵ ✵

For Wendy Schmalz, and in memory of her much
adored Emmet, a former shelter dog lucky enough
to know the comforts of home

Also, in memory of my childhood gentle giant,
Heidi; I loved her, drool and all

✵ ✵ ✵

Chapter 1

I might as well admit this straight up. I am not a dog person.

Never asked for one, pleaded for one, or begged for one.

Don't get me wrong. It's not that I dislike dogs or am scared of them or think the world would be a better place without them. It's just that I'm not the type of person who melts when she sees a basset hound or wants to rush over and hug any Lab she happens to cross paths with. When I see a dog, I usually don't give it a second glance.

And yet here I am, a certified non–dog lover, talking to a drooling Saint Bernard and scratching him behind his ear even though I'd much rather be inside, gulping down a can of cold grape soda. Especially after the steaming hot walk I just had coming home from school.

The dog's name is Killer. That is what my daddy decided he should be called. But he's lived with us for seven months now, and there's not a microscopic bit of meanness to be found in any of the big bones under his shaggy brown and white fur coat.

Daddy's second choice for a name wasn't any better for him: Cujo. Like the crazy dog that ripped people apart in that old movie.

A good name for him would have been something like Sweetie Pie. But I can't call him that because after all he is a boy, and he might take offense.

So I call him Beauregard.

"You like the name Beauregard, don't ya?" I ask.

His tail thumps dirt, kicking up dust as a response.

"Everyone should like their name. I like mine okay. Charlotte Hayes. Could be worse, I guess."

More tail thumping.

Having the name Killer is the least of this dog's problems, though. Unfortunately all *his* problems have somehow become my problems. I just wish I knew what to do about it.

Beauregard collapses to the ground, legs straight up, giant paws dangling in the air.

He's asking for a belly rub.

The white of his belly is covered with brown. He's been lying in dirt where the grass has been worn away. I really don't want a coating of dirt on my hands.

He stares up at me, pleading from his upside-down position. I look away and notice his water bowl is empty. It's been in the upper eighties today, and Beauregard has to be terribly thirsty, so I ignore his plea for a belly rub and pick up the empty bowl instead. I march over to the outside spigot and fill it to the brim. Sploshing water until my sneakers squish, I carry the bowl back and set it down. Beauregard jumps up and makes a nosedive into it, lapping water like crazy.

Even though it's technically the first week of fall, it feels more like the middle of summer here in Greater Oaks, West Virginia. I put my hands on top of my head, hoping to catch a faint breeze. My orange hair feels like an electric stovetop burner twisted all the way to high.

Beauregard pauses from his frantic drinking long enough to drool and give me a melancholy stare. Saint Bernards always look a bit sad with their droopy eyes and saggy mouths, but I know he'd at least look a little happier if I could bring him inside with me. He's been an outside dog since we've had him, but for the past four months he hasn't even had a moment's break from his chain.

Beauregard, finished with his water, rolls onto his back once more and lets out a whimper. I was hoping he'd forget about that belly rub. He whimpers again and sounds so pitiful that I go ahead and kneel beside him and begin stroking his dirty fur. I swish a few gnats away with my free hand.

"Life's not fair, is it, boy?" I ask.

He groans and flops from his back to his side and begins panting.

Life's not fair for Beauregard. It's not fair for me either. 'Cause I'm the one stuck taking care of him.

Chapter 2

"What's the use of getting a dog if it can't be inside with us?" I ask at dinner. I figure if Beauregard were inside with us, maybe taking care of him and spending time with him wouldn't seem like so much of a chore for me.

"That dog drools." Mama passes a bowl of mashed potatoes to my older sister, Agnes, and doesn't even bother looking at me. Instead she focuses her attention on cutting up her pork chop. "Can't have drool all over the house."

"Justin Lee drools," I say, pointing at my baby brother, who is sitting in his high chair, rubbing mashed potatoes into his tray. He makes a fist, smashing some into his mouth.

5

"It's different and you know it, Charlotte. Besides, Justin Lee won't always have a drool problem. He'll outgrow it. Killer won't," Mama says.

"Then why did we get a dog that drools? Lots of dogs don't drool, you know." I frown, cross my arms, and lean back in my chair until it's tipped on two rear legs.

"Don't ask me; ask your father. I wasn't the one that brought him home." Mama takes a moment to frown at Daddy, then gives me the eye. "And stop tipping your chair. You'll fall."

I know what her look means. It means, Shut up, Charlotte. Since Justin Lee was born, she only directs her attention at me when she wants me to be quiet and leave her alone.

Agnes elbows me hard and glares.

A few weeks ago Agnes told me a secret. She had listened in on a phone conversation between Daddy and Aunt Renee and found out Mama has something called postpartum depression. I'm supposed to pretend I don't know, though. Agnes overheard Daddy telling Aunt Renee he didn't want to worry the two of us kids about it.

Basically postpartum depression means Mama is almost always in a bad mood. Agnes told me not to make it any worse by pestering her. She said I need to take it easy on Mama, so she can get better. She's reminding me of that right now with her glare.

Mama's bad mood isn't helped by the fact that Justin Lee keeps her up practically all night long. Me and Agnes were good babies, Mama's said on more than one occasion. Slept through the night by the time we were four weeks old. But Justin Lee is another story. Still getting her up three, four times a night, even though he's nine months old.

I can't help noticing the dark circles under Mama's eyes, and suddenly I feel guilty for bothering her about Beauregard. Like Agnes, I'm worried about her too. She's somehow different from the mama I once knew. Before Justin Lee, Mama was full of spunk, always busy. Every morning she would throw on a pair of sweats and go running. She was a cross-country star back in high school and had kept up with it ever since. Now her running shoes just stay in the closet, gathering dust.

But Daddy doesn't look tired or depressed. And Mama did just tell me to ask him after all, so I do. "Daddy, why'd you get a dog that drools if it means he can't be kept in the house?"

"I've always liked the way Saint Bernards look. Drool or not, Killer's a beautiful dog," Daddy says. He quickly tries to change the subject away from drool and the house issue. "Did you know in Switzerland Saint Bernards have a history of rescuing people on snow-covered mountains? And they were bred by monks?"

I don't really care about their history. Getting a dog because of the way it looks, then totally ignoring it makes no sense to me. I mutter something to that effect, loud enough for Daddy to hear, and stare at my plate while pushing peas around with my fork.

"Honey, Killer's not ignored," Daddy says. "You're out there every day with him."

"That's because no one else bothers even so much as to fill his water bowl when it's empty." I stop pushing peas around and make a design in my mashed potatoes with my fork prongs.

"Taking on a few chores like that won't hurt you any," Daddy says gently.

"But—,"

Mama cuts me off. "Stop playing with your food now and eat, Charlotte." She rubs at her forehead like she has a headache.

Agnes kicks me under the table, and I catch a glimpse of Daddy looking at Mama. His eyes seem kind of sad and concerned, so I let out a sigh instead of arguing more.

Daddy goes to the kitchen sink and fills up his glass with water. He squints out the kitchen window and says, "There's my dog. Oh, he's a handsome one all right. Glad I didn't get one of those tiny hairless Chihuahuas, the ones with all the warts. They're sort of on the ugly side. Might have ruined my view."

When he sits back down at the table, his face is all red, like he's mighty angry, but he's smiling, so I know he is just trying hard to lighten the mood by being funny.

Daddy's face is always red, so it's hard to read him if you don't know him. He's a big guy, too. Fills an entire doorway. My friend Luanne calls him intimidating. She won't even make a peep when she comes over and he's around. But I've never been scared of him. Daddy's never given me anything to be scared about. He doesn't hit or yell. He just makes jokes.

Daddy takes a swig of water and reaches over to tousle my hair. "Charlotte, no need to worry about Killer. He's an outdoor dog. Nothing wrong with that. I love him, and he's got a good home here with us."

I want to blurt out, "You *used* to love him, and he *used* to have a good home," but I keep my mouth glued, not wanting to cause trouble. If I get on Mama's bad side again, I'll probably have to do dishes not only my week but Agnes's too.

What's funny is that Daddy was so proud of Beauregard when he first brought him home. Goodness, he was little then, just a couple of months old, and Daddy could still hold him in his thick arms. "Got him for a steal," he said.

A coworker of Daddy's originally bought the pup for five hundred dollars. Daddy said the man's wife threw such a fit over the purchase that she made him spend the night on the couch for an entire week. So the man decided to get rid of his newly acquired pet.

Now Daddy is the type always looking for a good deal, won't buy anything unless it's a bargain. His coworker offered the puppy for only two hundred dollars. Of course Daddy couldn't resist.

I thought Mama was going to make Daddy sleep on the couch, too, when he came home with Beauregard. She was whoppin' mad. Justin Lee was only two months old at the time, and Mama had said the last thing our house needed was another addition. "Those paws are already huge," she said, holding a squalling Justin Lee while Daddy cradled Beauregard like he was a human infant, too. "That's a Saint Bernard pup. He'll be two hundred pounds before you know it! Lord, what were you thinking!"

Daddy gave a look of mock surprise. "A Saint Bernard? Why, I thought this was one of them fancy shih tzus! A little dust mop you wouldn't even notice."

"Sheit-zu my foot," Mama said, swaying back and forth, trying to calm down Justin Lee. But she was doing it more in a mad way than a soothing one, and my brother just wailed louder. "And don't you dare expect me to take care of it!"

Daddy laughed at the words *shih tzu* and what Mama made it sound like. "I'll take good care of him. Don't worry your pretty little self about it," he said.

I have to say, for the first few weeks Daddy kept his word about taking care of Beauregard. He was always making over that dog. He built him a doghouse and painted it blue, just like our own house. It looked even nicer than our house, actually, since ours was faded and long overdue for a paint job. And Daddy could often be found outside with him, hugging him and whispering sweet nothings in his ear. Sometimes, when running errands, he'd take Beauregard with him. Beauregard always bounded into the car happily, like he was about to go on some grand adventure.

Agnes was pretty good to Beauregard, too, for a while. She'd take him off his chain and play with him, jumping around and getting him all wound up. He'd be barking and hopping like a giant rabbit, the motion making the loose skin around his mouth bounce up, and it almost looked like he was smiling. Then Beauregard got bigger and droolier, and Agnes started changing, too. She turned fourteen and got her first boyfriend. Daddy also moved on to the next thing that caught his fancy, a rusty, dented old Volkswagen Bug he had inherited from a great-uncle. He had big plans to restore it but only got as far as taking the engine half apart and painting the doors. It's been sitting unassembled in our garage since.

And me, well, as I said, I am not a dog person, so I was more than content to stand back and watch Daddy and Agnes with our growing puppy. Still, I couldn't help feeling sorry for him after they stopped spending time with him. And the last straw came when his food and water bowls began to be left empty. So I took over where they left off. I'm the one who feeds him, waters him, pets him, and scoops up the poop when piles start to take over. I can't say I enjoy it. But it's better than having to watch the poor dog suffer.

I chew at a piece of pork chop. I'm tempted to

keep on complaining about Beauregard's situation, telling them how he'd be much happier inside, even if it meant I'd be doing dishes Agnes's week. But then Daddy starts singing a silly made-up song about a hairless Chihuahua with warts that falls in love with a Saint Bernard. And soon Justin Lee is happily cooing along and Agnes has stopped glaring and Mama looks like maybe she might actually smile for once and I haven't seen her smile in such a long time.

So I don't have the heart to spoil the moment. Besides, complaining isn't going to accomplish anything. I tried complaining about the empty food and water bowls when I first noticed them to Daddy. He'd always say, "I'll get to it." But he never did. I need to think of a real plan.

Chapter 3

After another hot walk home from school, I go directly out back and take care of Beauregard. I'm really thirsty myself but set about filling his water bowl first. Then I sit next to him and do the belly rub thing. He pushes his head into my lap. Since I'm wearing shorts, I soon feel saliva dripping down my leg. I make a face, 'cause I'm repulsed, but don't move away.

I look over at the blue doghouse Daddy built. It doesn't offer much refuge anymore. Beauregard recently outgrew it. Sometimes he goes in, turns around, and lies down, but his head and front paws end up hanging out the front.

15

Just as I'm heading into the house, Luanne shows up.

"What are you frowning for?" she asks.

"I'm thirsty and hot, but I had to take care of Beauregard first," I say. "That dog would starve and die of dehydration if it weren't for me."

"Poor guy." Luanne walks over to Beauregard and lavishes soft strokes about his head. "How's my big baby?" she murmurs. Beauregard's tail starts swishing a mile a minute as he soaks up all the lovin' Luanne is giving him.

Luanne always dotes on Beauregard. She's a bona fide dog person. She even has her own dog, a little brown mutt, Jester, who gets to live inside. He has his own stuffed animal collection. Every time I see him he's got a blue bunny, tan bear, or yellow duck hanging from his mouth.

Unlike me, Luanne looks fresh and full of energy. Of course she lives between the school and my house, so she's already made a pit stop at her own home to cool off and get a drink.

"I'm going inside now," I tell her.

She gives Beauregard a final pat and follows me in.

Mama is in the kitchen, bent over, Justin Lee clutching her hands. He isn't walking on his own yet, so he and Mama are practicing.

I can't open the fridge quick enough to get out a can of grape soda. Air hisses as I push in the tab, and within seconds half the can is rolling around in my stomach.

Luanne is baby talking to Justin Lee in a singsong voice as he takes unsteady steps with Mama's help. He likes the attention from Luanne and starts grinning up a storm. Luanne tickles his stomach and, taking him from Mama, balances him on her hip. "You are getting heavy, mister!" she says.

Luanne is also a baby person. Me, I'm not so sure. Babies seem like even more work than dogs.

Last week Agnes insisted on teaching me how to do a French braid. I didn't really care to learn, but sometimes she can be real bossy, and it's not worth putting up a fight. Turns out I'm glad I didn't raise much of a stink, because once I got the knack of weaving hair into a tidy design, I kind of enjoyed it. So now I'm up in my room, brushing Luanne's hair so I can braid it up fancy.

Once I get everything all smoothed out, I lay the brush down on my bedspread. The brush is full of my orange hair, but now there's a few of Luanne's jet black hairs mixed in. Luanne's mother is from the Philippines, and Luanne takes after her; she looks nothing like her daddy, who is freckled and brownish blond. I divide Luanne's thick, shiny hair into three sections at the top and twist, gathering a little hair from each side as I go.

"She still hasn't talked," Luanne says.

"I know."

"She's different, don't you think?"

"Yes."

There really isn't much more to say about the new girl who appeared at our school two days ago—no one knows much about her—so we start talking about other stuff.

"Wish my mom would have a baby. Ouch!" Luanne suddenly jumps a bit.

"Sorry. Got to get it tight or it won't look right."
Luanne's an only child. I actually think she's lucky, but I don't say anything. Don't want to appear ungrateful for my own sister and brother.

"Mom said she's done, said she's happy with me and that one is enough. I'll just have to visit Justin Lee. He's so cute, isn't he?"

"I guess." I do the last twist to Luanne's hair and reach for a pink elastic band.

"I said the other night, if we can't have a baby in the house, then maybe we should get a puppy, but Mom said the same thing about Jester: one dog's enough."

"In my family one dog is too much," I say, sighing. "It's not that anyone intends to be mean to Beauregard. He's just . . . neglected. And lonely."

"He's such a good boy. So calm and gentle. I bet he wouldn't be any problem at all if you brought him in the house."

"That's what I tried to tell Mama and Daddy last night, but they wouldn't listen." I secure the pink hair band at the end of Luanne's braid and nudge her shoulder. "All done."

Luanne walks over to the mirror above my dresser and admires herself, turning her head from side to side. "Looks great."

"You can't even see it from the back," I say.

"There's no stray hairs sticking out, so it has to look good," she replies.

And it does. I don't think even Agnes can do a French braid as neat as I can. I've always been good with my hands, though. I'm real good at art. The best at drawing in my class.

I look out my bedroom window into the backyard below. Next door Mrs. Strickland is out, pulling some weeds in her flower bed. Beauregard is straining against his chain and wagging his tail, as if he'd like nothing more than to gallop over and give her a big slobbery kiss.

I wish I could fix Beauregard's problem as easily as I fixed Luanne's hair. We'd both feel better, I'm sure.

I wake up in the middle of the night, fuzzy-headed and trying to remember a dream. It was a nice dream,

I know that much for sure, and I want to continue it. Bits and pieces float groggily back. A family I don't know. Beauregard living with them. Him snuggled into a huge plaid doggy bed in the middle of their kitchen. Food and water bowls near the sink. Both bowls printed with his name. The letters were orange, and the room was painted yellow. Happiness. A feeling of happiness filled the room. And even though I wasn't in the kitchen with that family, I was hugged by that happiness, the feeling still clinging to me. The feeling starts to dissipate, though, and I try to sink into sleep again. But it won't come, and before I know it, I'm wide awake.

I know what I have to do. I have to find Beauregard a new home.

At breakfast Daddy is digging into a stack of pancakes, his favorite, and he looks pretty blissful, so I decide now would be as good a moment as any.

"Maybe we should give Killer away," I say.

Daddy lowers his fork, and his eyebrows arch in surprise. "Why should we do that? I love Killer." He raises his fork back up and points it at me. "You love that dog, too, don't you, Charlotte?"

"Not really."

"I've seen you with him. Petting him and talking to him. What kind of craziness are you up to? Have you lost your doggone mind?" He starts laughing. "Get it? Dog *gone* mind." He pierces a piece of pancake and pops it in his mouth.

Before I can say anything, Mama says, "I wouldn't mind getting rid of Killer."

With that, Agnes bursts into a crying fit. "You can't get rid of Killer!"

Mama and Daddy both seem puzzled by her sudden outpouring of emotion over Killer, but I'm not exactly surprised by the tears. Agnes's boyfriend called last night after dinner and broke up with her. I know she just wants an excuse to cry right now.

Daddy was teasing her about her sorrow when it happened. "You had a boyfriend?" he asked. "Are you talking about the kid who comes around here with the long hair in his eyes? I thought that was a new girlfriend."

"With a name like Tom!"

"Thought it was Jamie."

"That was my last boyfriend," she wailed, and proceeded to stomp up to her room.

At that point Daddy started to crack another joke, but Mama gave him a stern look, and he stopped superquick.

"Awww . . . she'll have a new boyfriend tomorrow," he said, shrugging.

Still pretending it's the thought of Killer being given away that has upset her so, Agnes daintily dabs at her eyes with a napkin, trying to get herself under control.

Daddy shoves another piece of pancake into his mouth. "See what you did, Charlotte, made your sister cry." He winks at me to show he doesn't really blame me and smiles. "Killer's a jim-dandy dog. Hasn't caused a moment's trouble. Doesn't dig. Doesn't bark unless he has a reason to. And I paid good money for him, too. Why on earth would I go and give him away?"

Mama answers the question for me. "He goes

through dog food like crazy. I buy a big bag at the grocery store every week. I'd much rather spend that money on other things, wouldn't you?"

Justin Lee squishes a piece of pancake into his eye. It sticks, like a monocle, and he laughs proudly.

Daddy starts laughing right along with him, ignoring what Mama has just said.

"Yeah, think of the money you could save if you didn't have that dog to feed," I say, trying to get the conversation back on track.

"Killer earns his keep. He's our watchdog. I'll tell you what, no one would dare break into our house at night. He's already big, over a hundred pounds easy. Can you imagine when he's full grown? That giant shadow of his in the moonlight and that big, deep bark? He's our security system. A bag of dog food a week is cheap for that." Daddy takes a piece of his own pancake, dabs it in syrup, and sticks it to his eye, copying Justin Lee's antics.

By now Justin Lee's pancake monocle has fallen off, so he squishes another piece of pancake into his eye and starts chuckling like crazy. Daddy erupts with laughter, too. And Agnes starts crying all over again. The room is a noisy ruckus, except for Mama and me.

Mama just looks at me and shakes her head at the commotion. Then she puts her head in her hands.

The good news is that I just found out Mama is on my side, that she wouldn't mind if Beauregard got a new home.

The bad news is, though, she's not the one who needs convincing.

After a few minutes Agnes finally regains her composure enough to talk about how elections are being held at the high school for the senior homecoming queen and class attendants. You can tell by her voice she thinks she has a good chance of representing the freshman class. She probably will. Agnes is very popular. And pretty.

Mama and Daddy become interested in the possibility of Agnes's winning the homecoming election, and it's apparent the conversation about Killer is over. I sigh and go through the breezeway at the back of the house. The dog food bag is kept in the corner there. At least Mama always remembers to buy food.

I scoop a small bucket full of food, carry it out, and dump the contents into Beauregard's food bowl. Every nugget is gone in about two seconds flat—he's a true chowhound. Then I fill up the water bowl, which I know will be empty when I get home. It's supposed to be another scorcher today.

Back when school started near the end of August, I made a point of asking Daddy to at least refill the water bowl when he came home for lunch. He said he would, but somehow he always forgets. Makes me so mad. How can he forget if Beauregard is right there outside the kitchen window as he eats his lunch? I wonder how he'd feel if he had to spend an entire day in the hot sun without anything to drink.

I take a few minutes to dutifully perform a morning belly rub. "What are we going to do, Beauregard?" I think about the dream I had about him happy in a new home.

Beauregard rolls from his back onto his stomach and looks at me as if he trusts me with all his heart.

"I'll keep trying. We'll find that family. Don't worry," I whisper to him.

Suddenly Beauregard sits up and starts pawing at his neck with a frenzy, like something suddenly bit him.

Fleas?

I bolt to my feet. Would Daddy want to put up with fleas?

I run back to the house. Agnes is putting the breakfast dishes into the sink, Mama is at the table, making out her grocery list, and Daddy is bouncing Justin Lee up and down on his knee.

"Beauregard has fleas!" I announce, waiting for their horrified reactions.

"That figures. He's a dog. Dogs and fleas go together like bees and honey," Daddy says, not even missing a bounce with Justin Lee.

"But what if one jumps on me and I come into the house. We could have a real infestation, all of us scratching and red from bites."

"Ewww, that's disgusting," Agnes says, wrinkling her nose. "I'm staying away from that dog!"

"See, maybe we should give him away after all," I say.

But all Daddy says is, "Mama, put a flea collar on your grocery list."

Mama doesn't look too happy to be adding to her list, but she jots it down anyway.

And before I know it, I'm on my way to school and my brain is still spinning, trying to come up with a decent plan.

I can't help thinking about fleas, too, and even though nothing's biting me, I stop to scratch myself.

Chapter 4

At lunch Luanne starts whispering about the new girl, who is sitting all alone at a table, with only her food tray for company. She is staring hard at her Johnny Marzetti, which she only picks at. It's almost as if she expects the lump of elbow noodles to carry on a conversation with her.

The new girl has been at our school for three days now. She is very beautiful with long blond hair that curls at the ends. She has long eyelashes and never smiles, never speaks. She is also rich. Most of the kids here at Perry Avenue Elementary live in town, all in small older houses with varying degrees of peeling paint and broken-down front porches. But

Grace Walters, the new girl, lives on the outskirts of town in a brand-new humongous brick house. It has a big arched window in the middle of the second story, and inside, you can see a gold chandelier hanging there. Our parents always slow down on Vinton Road to gawk at it. After you pass the house, all that can be seen for the next half mile is spanking white fence. And horses.

I guess because she's so weirdly beautiful and rich and hasn't spoken, we all treat her like she's an alien that's been dropped off by a spaceship or something. No one is mean to her, really. We just don't know what to say or do around her. So we stare at her and whisper.

All at once a firecracker of an idea flashes through my head. What better home for Beauregard than Grace's? Heck, if her family has horses, his size certainly shouldn't bother them any. He'd be living in the lap of luxury. And Grace seems like such a gentle girl. I couldn't imagine her yelling at him or mistreating him. I bet if I could talk Grace into wanting Beauregard, her father would offer like a thousand dollars for him. And that would be too good of a deal for my daddy to turn down, wouldn't it?

I pick up my tray. "I am going to sit with Grace Walters," I announce to Luanne and my other friends. They look stunned. A few of them gasp.

Luanne brushes her black bangs aside and says in a hushed voice, "You can't."

"Why not?" I ask.

"Well, I don't really know . . ." My friend looks very perplexed.

I leave her and the others to ponder my fate.

With a thunk I plunk my tray down across from Grace. She gives a startled jump, and I notice that all of a sudden there is dead silence coming from my classmates. I can feel everyone's collective eyeballs focusing on me and Grace, but I can't force any words from my throat. We look at each other for a split second, then just as quickly withdraw our gazes. Just when I think I can't stand it a moment more, Grace mumbles, "Thank you."

I sit down. "For what?"

"Coming over here."

"Oh . . . sure."

For the first time I see Grace smile. I notice her two front teeth are crossed. Badly.

She quickly covers her mouth with her hand and looks embarrassed. "I'm getting them fixed next month. Braces," she mutters through her fingers.

"That's okay. I've got a little gap between mine." I point at my front teeth.

"I guess we're opposites." She smiles again and doesn't seem as embarrassed.

She's not an alien at all, I decide. She's just shy.

I want to bubble over about Beauregard and how he would make the perfect pet for her family, but I figure that might scare her off. I need to ease my way into this somehow.

"Maybe you could come over to my house after school," I finally say. "I live nearby. We can just walk there." I won't even say a word about Beauregard. I'll have her over, she'll fall in love with him, and that will be that.

"I can't," Grace says. "My parents would want to meet your parents first. They have a rule about that."

"Oh . . ." I imagine her very proper parents meeting mine. Not good. Daddy with his red face and silly jokes. Mama all tired out. Our ramshackle old house. And dirty Beauregard chained up out back; he wouldn't make a good first impression on grown-ups, especially rich ones.

"Maybe you could come over to my house tomorrow," Grace says. "My mom could pick us up after school. I live outside town, so she drives me every day."

I nod. "That would be great."

My parents don't have any rules about meeting parents. Of course they practically know everyone in our town, since it's so small. Maybe me going over would work out better anyway, I decide. I could make up some sob story about how I have an allergy or something to Beauregard and that he needs a new home. And that would give me enough time to maybe give Beauregard a bath before they finally see him, so he would look pretty and fluffy and handsome for both Grace and her parents.

Grace gets shy again all of a sudden, and I am at a loss for what else to say. I motion to everyone at my old table to come join us and am met with frozen faces. I motion again, a little more desperately. Luanne finally comes through, lifting her tray and heading our way.

The others just sit and continue to stare as if they were witnessing the parting of the Red Sea.

Luanne says hello to Grace, but Grace just nods and starts acting fascinated with her Johnny Marzetti all over again. I shrug, and then Luanne, who is never one to be quiet for long, starts talking to me like we are the only two at the table.

I ask Mama if I can go over to Grace Walters's house after school tomorrow.

She's changing Justin Lee's diaper, and she stops mid wipe. She shoots a puzzled look my way and says, "I don't know any Grace Walters."

"The new girl," I say. "The one that lives in that big brick house on Vinton Road."

"Well, now I know where she lives, but I still don't know her family. I'm not real sure I want you going over there. At least not yet."

I couldn't believe it. "It will be all right," I say. "They're rich."

She frowns. "What does *that* matter?"

"Mama, please!" I say.

Mama sighs and shakes her head no.

"But why?"

Agnes comes into the room. "What are you bothering Mama about now?" she says. "Can't she change Justin Lee's diaper in peace?"

"Mama won't let me go over to the new girl's house. The one on Vinton Road."

"Oh, I love that house!" Agnes forgets about scolding me for a moment and clasps her hands together. "It looks like it belongs in a magazine!"

"But I don't know anything about the family," Mama says firmly. She picks up a freshly diapered Justin Lee. He winds a chubby hand around her hair and pulls. She says nothing further, just untangles her hair from his clutches. I can tell the discussion is over as far as she is concerned.

Luckily Daddy walks into the room. He had gotten off work early. Some kind of breakdown in equipment at the ball bearing plant that needed to be fixed, he says, so they sent everyone home except for the repair crew. He overheard the last thing Mama said. "You don't know anything about what family?" he asks.

Mama explains, and he ends up coming to my rescue. Just so happens that his boss is a real good friend of Grace's dad. Daddy has even met Mr. Walters a few times, so Mama finally relents.

With that settled, Daddy scoops Justin Lee up and starts swooping him through the air while making airplane noises.

I feel like swooping through the air, too. Beauregard is on his way to being saved, I'm sure. I figure Grace and her parents will be coming to get him maybe in a day or two. I need to get him gussied up!

"Mama, can I use the garden hose to give Killer a bath?" I ask.

Mama eyes me suspiciously. "Why do you want to give him a bath?"

Daddy interrupts his verrrrooom-rooooming, causing Justin Lee's plane engine to come to an abrupt standstill. "The fleas, remember?" he says.

"Yeah. I thought a bath would be a good idea because of the fleas," I say quickly.

"Oh, that reminds me, I got Killer a flea collar. The package is on the countertop in the kitchen. Put it on him after you're done." Mama yawns, looking like she could fall asleep on the spot.

"Mama," Agnes says, "why don't you and Daddy go out to dinner tonight? Just the two of you. I'll watch Justin Lee."

"That sounds like a good idea," Daddy says. He hands off Justin Lee to Agnes like it is a done deal.

But Mama shakes her head no. "I'm a mess. Don't even have the energy to fix myself up. Besides, I've already gotten some hamburger out to thaw for meat loaf."

"Well, I'll just keep Justin Lee busy for a while before dinner then," Agnes says.

"And heck, I can fix the meat loaf," Daddy says. "Just a little ketchup, Worcestershire, and bread crumbs mixed in with the hamburger, right?"

"There's eggs, too. And onions." Mama doesn't

look like she quite trusts Daddy's cooking abilities but agrees to go ahead and get the recipe out for him.

So with Agnes looking after Justin Lee, Daddy putting together meat loaf, and me with plans to get Beauregard all spiffy, Mama will have a quiet house and alone time for a bit. Maybe that will be even nicer than dinner out.

I run upstairs to the bathroom. Lined up on the bathtub edge we have baby shampoo, Daddy's Head & Shoulders for dandruff, Mama's generic discount stuff, which I also use, and Agnes's strawberry essence. I decide on the strawberry essence. Wouldn't hurt if Beauregard smelled scrumptious too.

Soon I'm spraying Beauregard with cold water from the hose. I'm surprised he isn't straining at the chain to break away since a lot of dogs don't like baths, but he truly seems to enjoy getting all wet. Probably a relief from the heat. Once he is dripping water from head to tail, I squeeze out a good amount of strawberry essence and work it in. He stands there patiently as I rub away, soap foaming up from between my fingers. He looks like a bubbly abominal snowman. Then he starts to shake. Blobs of white froth come flying at me.

"Just who is giving who a bath?" I ask, laughing.

He stops shaking, becomes still as a statue, and gives me a look like: Who me? What did I do?

I rinse him off, take a beach towel to him, and then stand back to admire how white his white patches look and how shiny his dark patches are. Then I sniff the air around him.

Strawberry essence.

Perfect.

Chapter 5

As soon as I'm done with Beauregard's bath and come into the kitchen, I find Daddy sticking the meat loaf into the oven. Mama is reading a magazine at the table, and I wonder if she did more supervising of the meat loaf than reading. Since the meat loaf will take a while to cook and there's time before dinner, Daddy announces he's going to hit up a yard sale going on down the street. I ask if I can tag along, and he says, "Sure."

Usually you think of women sorting through used clothes and jewelry or hunting for antiques, but Daddy loves yard sales more than anyone I know.

Mama just looks at the two of us as we head out the door and shakes her head. Daddy always manages to bring home something interesting when he visits a yard sale. Unfortunately most of the time interesting equals useless, and our closets, cabinets, and garage are bursting at the seams with his "finds."

"Maybe I should bring Killer?" I say as soon as we get outside. "The walk would help him finish drying off from his bath."

"He's too big for you to handle," Daddy says. "He'd end up dragging you or getting away. He could run out in front of a car and get hit."

"You could take him then," I say. "He won't get away from you. You're strong."

"I need my strong arms to carry things home from the yard sale. Who knows what all we'll find?" he says, his voice full of hope.

Daddy puts his arm around my shoulder and hums a silly country song until we reach a house with tables set up outside and stacked high with what looks like junk: paperbacks, pans and skillets, flower pots and vases.

"All the good stuff is probably already gone," Daddy mumbles. "Should have stopped here during lunch, but I offered to make a grocery run for Mama; we were out of laundry detergent, and she had to do a load. Oh, well."

Daddy picks up a cordless drill and inspects it. Now Daddy already has a cordless drill, one that works perfectly fine. "Eight dollars," he says. "Bet I can talk them down to five."

I take a gander at the stuff on the table behind Daddy. "Hey, look, oil paints!" I say.

Daddy puts down the drill and turns around. "That's interesting," he says. He picks up one of the tubes of paint and studies the cardboard sign taped to the table: LEARN TO PAINT FOR $15.00—INCLUDES OILS, CANVAS, AND BOOK.

"Kind of expensive, though, don't you think?" He puts the tube down and flips through the book like he's still considering purchasing the items but then shrugs and goes back to inspecting the drill again.

Someone moves in next to me, and a woman's voice yells, "Will you look at that, Drew? Oil paints! The how-to book is atrocious. People call that art? But the oil paints are top-notch and barely used. Plus there is blank canvas, too. You know what I would pay for all that at an art supply store? Over a hundred dollars. Easy! I can't believe they're only asking fifteen!"

Daddy spins around, and I take a good look at who the voice came from. It's a well-dressed woman in a summery, flowing, flowery dress and hat. And the man with her has on dress slacks and a shirt with a fancy emblem. His hair is all slicked back. Out-of-towners, my best guess. The woman is eyeing the items on the table, her chin cupped between a finger and thumb.

With what happens next you'd think Daddy had suddenly donned a Superman cape. He swoops in and grabs the oil paints, canvas, and book as if he's on a mission to snatch a child from the window of a burning building.

The woman starts to sputter but can't quite get her words out she is so shocked.

"Come on, Charlotte, let's go pay for these," he says, his arms full.

I'm dreadfully embarrassed by Daddy's behavior. My cheeks feel all hot and pink, but at the same time, I can't help smiling a teeny bit. I've always wanted to learn to paint with oils. At school we just have baby-ish yellow, blue, and red finger paints, or the cheap watercolors that come in a little strip. These are the real deal.

After dinner Daddy clears a small empty space in the breezeway, just enough room for a person to stand. There are three empty canvas pieces he purchased, and he props one up on the windowsill, turning it into a makeshift easel. I watch from the doorway, interested but just a little disappointed. I'd sure like to use those paints myself, but apparently he has a creative streak he needs to satisfy, too.

He opens the book and reads for a few minutes. "Supposed to use a palette to mix paint colors." He frowns. "Heck, there are eight tubes here, and the colors look fine to me. Why would I bother mixing them?"

Daddy thumbs through the book and finally settles on a page. "This looks good," he says more to himself than to me. He grabs an old wood chair with a broken-back spindle from the corner of the breezeway and lays the opened book on it.

I walk over to see what he has picked out to paint. Given Daddy's sense of humor, I expect poker-playing dogs. But it is a pretty picture of colorful flowers arranged in a yellow vase.

"Think Mama will like this?" he asks.

I nod.

"She's been saying for a long time that she wants to find something to hang on the wall over the couch."

"That will look nice," I say. Since Daddy is doing this for Mama, I force myself to swallow the disappointment I've been feeling over not being able to use the paints myself. With Mama being down in the dumps, I'm all for anything to make her feel better.

"Do me a favor, Charlotte. I need turpentine to clean the brushes, it says. Go out to the garage. I should have a can stored under my workbench. I need an old towel, too."

I go after the towel first. The linen closet is upstairs, across from the bathroom. Mama is running water for

Justin Lee's bath, while he sits on the floor beside her, chewing on a hard rubber rattle in the shape of a horse.

I poke my head into the bathroom. "Daddy needs an old towel to clean paintbrushes with."

"Should be a dark green one, has a few holes in it. Give him that one." Mama puts her fingertips in the water, gauging the temperature. She shakes her head. "I can't believe he bought paints. Of all things." She doesn't sound too happy.

"He's painting a picture for you," I say, trying to cheer her up.

But she just stares at me blankly and starts undressing Justin Lee.

Daddy used to make her laugh. Even when he wasn't trying to be funny, she found him amusing. Like when we went to Cousin Bernadette's wedding and half the people there were doing a line dance called the hustle. Daddy was so proud he knew all the steps that he was extra-exuberant in his dancing, but he went left when he should have gone right and ended up starting a chain reaction that knocked a whole row of people down. Mama laughed so hard she ended up on the ground, too, even though she wasn't in the line that fell over like bowling pins.

Mama has always been firm and strict. But underneath it all she had a sense of humor that somehow always managed to shine through. It's been forever since I've seen a true smile on her face, not just a hint of one. I think the last time was in response to Justin Lee giving his first smile. She was so excited about that. But it was almost like when he began smiling, he stole all her smiles from her. I know Justin Lee is not to blame, though. Agnes told me it has something to do with Mama's hormones after giving birth.

I rifle through the linen closet, looking for the towel. Worrying about Beauregard is bad enough. But I've got Mama on my mind, too. I find the green towel with holes and tuck it under my arm. At least Beauregard shouldn't be a concern much longer. He's clean, shampooed, scented, and ready to go. Pretty soon he'll be living the high life with Grace Walters.

I head for the garage in search of turpentine.

Chapter 6

The next day Luanne and I sit with Grace again at lunch. I try to get Grace talking, but when I ask her a question, she only gives one- or two-word answers and seems to be hypnotized by her fork. Luanne keeps on looking longingly at our old lunch table, where Roxanne, Madison, and Becca sit gabbing away. I'd rather be sitting there, too, but Beauregard is counting on me.

Mrs. Walters happens to be blond and pretty, like Grace, except I notice her teeth are perfectly straight in front. Maybe she had braces like the ones Grace is going to get. I settle into the leather seat of the green SUV she's driving. It smells fresh and clean and perfumy, and I breathe in deeply. Our car is littered with Justin Lee's Cheerios and smells faintly of cigarettes. Daddy bought the car—for a good deal, of course—from a cousin of his who chain-smokes. Mama tried airing it out by driving with the windows open, but the smell still lingers.

Mrs. Walters keeps the drive from being too quiet by asking me all kinds of things: how long I've lived in Greater Oaks (forever), what my favorite subject is (art, which unfortunately we only have once a week), where my parents work (Mama at home; Daddy at Greater Oaks's only factory, Denmar's ball bearing plant). I mention Daddy's boss's name, and she says how he is a good friend of theirs and how he was the one who told them about the property on Vinton Road for sale. How they wanted to move from Pittsburgh, PA, to a place in the country, and since Grace's dad was some sort of consultant, they were able to relocate wherever they wanted. Grace just stares out the window through all this. I don't mention Beauregard. Yet.

I walk inside the front door and stand under the big gold chandelier, resisting the urge to let a big "wow!" escape.

I've never seen a house like this before. The living room to my right is bigger than the whole first floor of my house. Heavy stuffed furniture in greens and golds and reds fills it up. It's a king-size house fit for a king-size dog, I think happily. Plenty of room for Beauregard.

All at once a huge shaggy black thing comes bounding out of nowhere and nearly knocks me over. I steady myself, and for a moment I get real concerned about my plan. They already have a dog! But then I eye the cavernous dining room to my left. Heck, this place could house a whole passel of dogs, no problem.

Grace kneels and greets the dog. She asks him to sit and shake and he promptly obeys. "He's really smart," she tells me proudly.

Mrs. Walters bends over and hugs the black dog. He gets all excited and starts jumping around, then stops and leans against her leg. She laughs. "Did you miss me, Figaro? I wasn't gone that long." She hugs him again.

I take this as good news. Grace and her mom obviously like dogs! All I have to do is give them my sob story about being allergic to Beauregard, and he'll have a new home in no time.

Then it occurs to me. I should be sneezing right now if I'm allergic to dogs, since Figaro is near me. But if I start sneezing because I'm allergic, then I'll have to leave. Which means I won't have a chance to talk to Grace and her mom about Beauregard.

Hmm . . . maybe instead of *me* being allergic, I can just say that Justin Lee is. That would actually be even better because he is a helpless baby. More sympathy involved.

"Nice dog," I comment. I really don't want to pet Figaro any more than I want to pet Beauregard, but I do anyway. I smile and do my best to pretend that petting dogs is something I truly enjoy. He starts leaning against me, like he did with Mrs. Walters earlier.

"We have a dog at home. A purebred Saint Bernard. Very friendly," I say. "Gentle as can be. And so handsome! It's such a shame we have to sell him." I shake my head and give my best mournful look.

"Why do you have to sell him?" Mrs. Walters asks, falling right into my trap.

"Oh, my baby brother is deathly allergic to dogs. Doctor said we have to do something right away. We keep the dog outside now, but that isn't enough. Justin Lee still has trouble breathing."

"Oh, that's so sad," says Grace. "I'd about die if we had to sell Figaro."

"You know, I've always loved Saint Bernards," Mrs. Walters says wistfully.

I smile real big, and it's all I can do to keep from hopping up and down with excitement over how things are working out.

"I'd buy him in a minute, but I'm afraid I'm terribly allergic to dogs, too."

My heart skips a beat as I try to register the

words I've just heard Grace's mom utter.

Figaro leaves me and goes over to Mrs. Walters, nudging her hand for some more attention. She pats his head. "Figaro, here, is as close to hypoallergenic as a dog can be," she says. "He's a labradoodle, a cross between a Lab and a standard poodle. If bred right, they don't shed. Maybe if you find a home for your Saint Bernard, I can give your parents information about the breeder we got him from. You do have to be careful with who you buy one from; not all Labradoodles are shed-free."

I stand there, my mouth gaping open.

"Grace, why don't you be a good hostess and show Charlotte your room?" Mrs. Walters says.

Grace suddenly looks kind of panicky and shy, but she goes ahead and leads me up one side of a double curved stairway with a dark wood banister. When we get to her room, we just stand there staring at each other.

I feel a compulsion to say something, so to my surprise I hurl out the words "Justin Lee doesn't really have an allergy." My hand flies up to my mouth. I'm not used to telling lies, I guess.

"Why did you say he did then?" Grace frowns. She doesn't look mad, just confused.

I tell her about my problem with Beauregard. How I have to take care of him when I don't even like dogs. And how he deserves a better life. "He is chained up all the time," I say. "I think he's horribly lonely."

"Well, I have a lot in common with Beauregard then. I'm lonely, too," Grace says. She tells me how much she misses her old friends and how scared she's been that she won't make any new ones here. She says she loved living in Pittsburgh and isn't so sure about the move here. She doesn't sound snotty or stuck-up about it at all, just a little sad.

"Moving would be tough," I say. "I'd hate to have to say good-bye to Luanne, so I understand what you mean."

"I was so happy when you and Luanne sat with me at lunch yesterday and today." Grace leans against the white post of her canopy bed. "But then I froze up. I was afraid I would say something wrong or stupid and then you wouldn't like me, I guess."

"Well, Luanne and I sometimes say stupid things to each other." I laugh, sitting on her bed. "And we're still friends. So you have nothing to worry about."

Before long Grace is sitting on the bed with me, and we are leaning in close and talking and laughing, and there is no room for any silence between us.

When Mama comes to pick me up a couple of hours later, Mrs. Walters takes a few minutes to make small talk. All of a sudden I get worried she might mention Justin Lee's allergies. Mama's big on not telling lies. And Mrs. Walters might wonder what kind of new friend her daughter had if she discovered I told a whopper within minutes of meeting her. But luckily Mama had left the baby home with Agnes, and he was never brought up. As we are leaving and walking down the sidewalk, though, Mrs. Walters calls out, "I'll keep an ear open for someone who wants a Saint Bernard."

Once we're in the car, Mama just shakes her head. "Charlotte, your daddy isn't about to let go of that dog. And I've got more important things to do than force the issue. You need to drop the subject. Okay?"

I look down at my hands and mutter, "Okay," not wanting to cause Mama any trouble by arguing with her. But I just told another lie. I'm not about to give up yet. Besides, Mama said before that she wouldn't mind getting rid of Beauregard. If I can find a way to do it without stirring up waves, maybe it will make her happy, too.

When we get home, I rush out back to get Beauregard's water bowl filled. Since I went straight to Grace's house after school, he has had to wait an extralong time for me. After he laps up plenty of fresh water and I give him his expected belly rub, I decide to try to teach him to shake hands, like Grace's dog, Figaro. I figure it will make him more desirable as a pet, so he can get a good home. Just because he can't go live with Grace and her family doesn't mean no one else is out there who would be willing to buy him.

I push his hind end down so he is sitting.

"Shake!" I say. I reach down and grab a huge front paw, pumping it up and down. "Good boy!"

Beauregard cocks his head to the side, like he doesn't

56

know quite what to make of this new activity.

I repeat the process over and over again.

Finally I try saying, "Shake," without grabbing his paw, fully expecting him to lift it on his own. But his big old paw stays firmly planted on the ground. He wrinkles his brow, locking eyes with me. "I don't get it," he seems to be saying.

"Oh, come on now," I say, disappointed.

I think for a moment, then dash back to the house and into the kitchen. I grab about five gingersnap cookies, Daddy's favorite, from a package in the pantry and beat a quick path back to Beauregard.

I still grab his paw for him when I say, "Shake," but this time, as soon as I tell him, "Good boy," I hold out half a gingersnap. The way he wolfs down food in his bowl, I'm half afraid he'll take my fingers with the cookie, but he sniffs it first, then gently curls his lips around it and takes it from my hand. He sticks out his tongue to give his mouth a lick and stares at me like I presented him with the most wondrous treasure in the whole wide world.

By the time I'm on the third gingersnap, he raises

his own paw without me grabbing it. I'm so proud of him I hug him after he gobbles down his treat.

He still smells like his bath, and I linger with my face pressed against his neck for a few moments.

I love the smell of strawberries. Maybe I should start using Agnes's shampoo, too.

Chapter 7

On Friday morning our sixth-grade teacher, Mrs. Delenor, greets us with a huge smile on her face, almost like she has a secret she can't wait to share. As soon as the bell rings and we all get seated, she goes over to her desk and picks up a photo frame. She turns it out, facing us, so we can all see the picture inside. It's a little dog, white and fluffy. Some of the girls in class start oohing and aahing.

"This is Snowflake," Mrs. Delenor says. "She's a new member of my family. Did any of you read in the paper last week about the animal shelter that opened on Fenton Street?"

A few kids say they did. I read only the funnies, so

this is news to me. The funnies are Daddy's favorite part of the paper, too. Agnes likes the horoscope and advice columns. I think Mama is the only one in the house who really reads the newspaper for news.

"Well," Mrs. Delenor continues, "I adopted Snowflake from the shelter yesterday." She takes the framed picture and gives it to a boy near the front of the class, so it can be passed around for everyone to get a closer look. "I talked to the shelter manager and found out it needs a lot of help to keep everything up and running. It really depends on donations from the community. So I thought the shelter might make a good service project for our class."

Mrs. Delenor gets a pile of handouts from her desk and starts to pass them out. "I want everyone to collect the items on this list: used or new leashes or collars, dog food, cat food, cat litter, paper towels, blankets, trash bags, and also aluminum cans, which the shelter can turn in for recycling money. Bring the collected items to school a week from Monday; that will give you plenty of time to gather your items.

We will then make a short field trip to the shelter to present the donations. I've also arranged a tour."

The framed picture of Mrs. Delenor's new dog makes its way to me. Snowball is a cute dog, I guess, and pretty lucky she has a home with Mrs. Delenor. I instantly wish I could take Beauregard to the shelter and find him a home. But there's no way Daddy would give his two-hundred-dollar dog away to any shelter, that much is for sure.

At lunch me, Grace, and Luanne sit together again. I wonder if Grace will get nervous and clam up like before, but she leans over and whispers, "Maybe the shelter is the answer to your problem."

Luanne overhears her. "What problem?"

I explain to her about how I've decided to solve Beauregard's problems (and mine) by finding him a better home.

"You've been complaining to me about having to take care of him, but you never told me about trying to find him a new home." Luanne seems a little hurt that Grace knows something she didn't.

"Well, I was thinking maybe Grace's family would

buy him, but it didn't work out. Her mother's allergic," I say.

Luanne looks even more hurt. "Why didn't you ask if my family would buy him?"

"'Cause you just told me the other day that your mom said Jester was enough."

"Oh. Right." Now Luanne looks a little sheepish for acting jealous. She takes a sip of her milk through her straw, then says, "So now you're thinking about taking him to the shelter?"

I shake my head. "Daddy wouldn't allow it. He wants to keep Beauregard."

"Why?" Luanne asks. "He doesn't really seem to care about that dog."

I shrug. "He says he loves him. I guess it's sort of like . . . like he gets distracted and doesn't stop to think about Beauregard much. Plus Beauregard's an expensive dog that he got for a good deal. And Daddy thinks he'll scare robbers away from the house."

Grace starts paying attention to Luanne and asking her questions. I think she feels bad that Luanne's feelings got hurt a minute ago. Pretty soon the two are talking up a storm. Grace, who seemed so shy at first, is now a chatterbox. She's just like a windup doll needing her key turned, and I guess me being friendly to her yesterday, when I visited, is what finally did the trick. Right now she is smiling, showing her crossed teeth, and she looks much more relaxed and comfortable than I've ever seen her at school.

So even though I wasn't able to help Beauregard by approaching her, I do feel kind of good because at least I was able to help her.

Daddy spends an hour or so after dinner working on his painting for Mama while I watch. He explains to me that oil painting is done in layers and that oil paint dries real slow, so you don't actually have to finish the painting right away. What he has done so far doesn't look much like the picture in the how-to book, but he doesn't seem discouraged yet.

I'm not discouraged about my project either. Sooner or later I'll find Beauregard a home. Just got to come up with the right idea.

Chapter 8

When I go out to feed Beauregard on Monday morning, I can see my breath come out in steamy puffs. Overnight we have gone from summerlike weather to fall. The grass is crunchy with frost. I dump the dog food into the bowl and wrap my jacket tightly around me. We got Beauregard near the beginning of spring. I started caring for him when summer was about to hit. It was bad enough doing it in the ninety-plus-degree heat, I don't want to think about doing it in the snow and cold that will be coming this winter.

However, with the plan I came up with over the

weekend, I don't think I'll have to worry about taking care of him much longer.

Beauregard, done scarfing down his food, rolls over for a belly rub. My hands are freezing, so I don't mind obliging today. The friction with his fur warms my hands.

Finally I stand, and he sits up. "Shake," I say, wondering if he'll remember. And he does! He lifts his paw, and I take it in my hand. I don't have any gingersnaps to give him, but he seems content with me telling him, "good boy." And he really is good. Smart, too. There's no denying that. It makes me feel a little sad that I'm not a dog person.

The whole day long at school all I can think about is my plan. I want to share it with Grace and Luanne at lunch, but I decide to wait until everything's done and over with and a success. Then I'll tell them what happened.

Instead of going straight out back to fill Beauregard's water bowl once I get home, I go inside. Mama looks especially tired. Justin Lee kept her up half the night, she says. He's taking a nap, so she tells me she's headed upstairs to take one, too. I feel bad for her and wonder how long this postpartum depression stuff lasts. Surely not too much longer. I just want Mama back, the mama who brushed my hair away from my face and always had time to ask me about school when I came home.

Anyway, Agnes is at some high school club meeting, I know, and won't be home till later.

So now's the perfect time for my plan.

As Mama climbs the stairway, I tell her I'm going over to Luanne's for a bit. She nods and tells me to be home by dinner.

I don't go over to Luanne's, though. I get a piece of rope from the garage, go to the backyard, unclip Beauregard from his chain, thread the rope through his collar, and we're off.

Chapter 9

The handout Mrs. Delenor gave us said the shelter was located at 258 Fenton Street. I figure it will be about a fifteen-minute walk. Over the weekend I realized this shelter was meant to be. I mean, it opened just in time for Beauregard. It was like a sign from above. I just have to be a little devious about it, that's all.

Beauregard is pulling hard at the rope, and he's practically prancing he's so happy to be going somewhere. The rope starts slipping through my hands, even though I'm gripping it with all my strength, and it hurts.

"Ouch!" I shriek. I think about what Daddy

said—that Beauregard's too strong for me to handle—
and I imagine how terrible it would be if he got away
from me and got hit by a car.

I yell at Beauregard, and he slows down a bit. He
cocks his head, looks at me like he is suddenly aware
I am traveling with him, and begins to stay closer to
my side. I keep talking to him, so he won't start pulling again. He seems to understand he shouldn't pull,
and I feel a bit more confident having him on my
makeshift leash.

Here is my devious plan:

I figure if I show up at the shelter and tell them
Beauregard belongs to me and my family and that we
don't want him anymore, they'd want to call Mama
and Daddy to make sure it's all right. And of course
it wouldn't be, and I'd be in big trouble. But if I show
up with Beauregard and tell them he's a stray I found,
well, what can they do but take him in and find him
a home?

The shelter is located between Rhonda's Cut and
Curl, where Mama, Agnes, and I get our hair done,

and a store that sells tires. I recognize the building. There used to be a pizza shop there, but it went out of business.

Across the street is a house Mama is in love with. It's one of the biggest in town but is pretty run-down–looking. Mama has always said if she won the lottery, she'd buy it and fix it up to its former glory. Our old house wouldn't be much fixed up, she says, but that one would be something else. Some old lady lives there now, I guess, who doesn't get out a lot. Mama told me that she had plenty of money to make the house look good and that it was such a pity she didn't.

I wish we'd win the lottery. I wish Mama could buy her dream house and fix it up. Maybe then she'd be happy enough to put on her running shoes every day.

I open the door, and Beauregard stands back, like he's not sure he should go in.

"Come on," I say, and I almost slip up and call him by name, but I stop myself right in time. He's a stray, I remind myself, so he doesn't have a name.

Beauregard follows me in and starts sniffing the floor, smelling other dog scents, I'm sure.

There is a lady at the front desk who greets me. She's got short, straight brown hair and she's wearing a dark green T-shirt, with the shelter logo, and jeans.

"What have we here?" she asks. She comes from behind the counter and leans over to pet Beauregard. He wags his tail and stops sniffing the ground. Instead he begins sniffing her.

"I found him running loose in the streets," I tell her. "Almost got hit by a car. Poor thing." I shake my head in mock concern.

The lady looks Beauregard over real good. "Hmm . . . he has a collar but no tags. Doesn't look underweight." She rakes her fingers through his hair. "Fairly clean, too. He doesn't look like a stray, but you never know."

I instantly regret giving him that bath; maybe I should have rubbed him down with dirt before coming here.

"If he does belong to someone, they have three days to pick him up." She smiles at me. I notice her nametag. It says "Kathleen." "Well, let's get him all set up. You can come along, if you like," she says.

Kathleen takes Beauregard's rope, and I follow her through a small room that has ten small cages. Six are empty, but four contain cats. They start meowing at us and rubbing back and forth against the fronts of their cages. We then enter a hallway and go through a door to the left where there are five large kennel cages set up, all empty.

"This is where we keep the dogs that have just come in. After three days, if no one claims them and if they seem reasonably healthy and social, we move them into the adoption room. I just moved two dogs into the adoption room this morning, so this guy here that you found will be our only resident for now." She opens the wire door to the nearest kennel and ends up actually having to shove Beauregard in from behind because he wants to stay right by my side. He looks mighty puzzled and kind of hurt when she closes the door on him. He drops his head, paws at the metal grating, and whimpers.

I feel a little bad for Beauregard, but I know better

things are in store for him: a nice home of his own. I remember the yellow kitchen walls and fancy printed dog bowls from my dream. I smile, and a real sense of accomplishment sinks in. I've done exactly what I set out to do.

"It was so nice of you to bring him here. We'll take good care of him," Kathleen tells me. "Would you like to see our other dog room?"

I nod, to be polite.

Down the other side of the hall is the adoption room. As soon as we step inside, I want to cover my ears. Terrible barking and yapping. I count five dogs, but it sounds more like thirty. They are all jumping against the sides of their kennels.

"I shouldn't have brought you in here," Kathleen says, raising her voice above the commotion. She grins. "You'll probably want to take them all home!"

I nod again. I don't bother telling her I'm not a dog person.

Chapter 10

I squeeze some ketchup onto my hamburger and take a bite. Daddy and Agnes have been home for nearly two hours now, and no one has even noticed that Beauregard's gone. Maybe no one ever will. It wouldn't surprise me. Agnes is telling Mama and Daddy about the dress she wants for homecoming. There is a mall about an hour away, and her friend Janelle's mother took the two of them shopping there last night. "The dress is royal blue," she says, "and it fits perfect. Plus it's on sale."

"How much?" Daddy asks.

When she tells him, he pretends to choke on a french fry, even though the price doesn't really sound that bad.

"Daddy, I have to look good," Agnes says. "I'm going to be the freshman attendant to the homecoming queen."

"Your mama has a few dresses in her closet," Daddy says, grinning. "You can just wear one of hers. There's that striped one she wore when she was pregnant with Justin Lee. Just wrap a belt around it, and you're good to go!"

"Oh, Daddy." Agnes is not amused. She rolls her eyes. "The dress is forty percent off. It's a good deal."

"Well, I guess it's important that you look good. Maybe if I stop eating for about a month, we can afford it," he says, winking and patting his stomach.

"That will be the day," Agnes says. She laughs, knowing the dress is hers. She gets up and gives him a hug. "Thanks, Daddy."

Mama sighs. "I'll run you up to the mall tomorrow."

"Oh, you don't have to, Mama. Janelle and her mother are making another trip tomorrow. Janelle couldn't decide between two dresses when we were there last night. I'll just get the money from you before I leave." Agnes is so happy she practically skips out of the room.

Daddy goes over to the sink to refill his water glass. He stares out into the backyard. He turns the spigot off and takes a sip from his glass.

"Where's Killer?" he suddenly sputters, water spraying from his mouth and dribbling down his chin.

Mama walks over to the window.

"Where on God's green earth is Killer?" Daddy repeats.

I join Mama and Daddy and stare out the window with a perplexed look on my face, too, so no one will be suspicious. Only Justin Lee is left sitting at the table.

"Someone up and stole him," Daddy says. "He's a purebred. Worth some money." He shakes his head. "I'll be doggone . . ."

This time Daddy doesn't even realize the funny wordplay when he says "doggone." There's just silence.

Chapter 11

I snuggle into the covers, pleased as can be with myself.

Daddy is far from pleased by what happened today, though. He grew more and more livid as the evening wore on. "Can't believe someone took Killer. It's awful to look out the kitchen window and to have him gone like that. Makes the backyard look empty somehow. I miss knowing he's there. Dadblameit all."

Now, Daddy is hard to make mad. He makes a joke over nearly everything. But this has really gotten his goat. He even let a curse word fly, and Mama had to give him her "look" to settle him down. Daddy was so upset he didn't even work on his flower painting, like he has gotten into the habit of doing after dinner.

The room is dark, and I close my eyes, but I'm not sleepy in the least. All at once that pleased feeling disappears and instead I keep on seeing Beauregard's sad, puzzled face. I feel a little sting in my chest. I hope he doesn't have to spend too much time in the shelter. I say a little prayer that after his three-day waiting period is over, he will find a home lickety-split. Then I imagine him sleeping on a plaid doggy bed in a yellow kitchen, and I feel better.

The next morning, out of habit, I head for the breezeway after breakfast.

Duh. No dog out there to feed this morning. Hip-hip hooray! I do a little jig to celebrate.

By the time I get to school, I'm busting to tell Grace and Luanne about how I solved the Beauregard problem. But Mrs. Delenor keeps us busy from the time we're seated until lunch.

Finally, as we sit down with our trays of fish sticks and tartar sauce, I whisper, "I did it."

"Did what?" Grace asks.

"Got rid of Beauregard. He's on his way to a good home." I explain my plan and how it went off without a hitch.

All at once Luanne's eyes grow wide and panicky. "Oh, Charlotte, no! You didn't!"

"What's wrong?" I dab my fish stick in a blob of tartar sauce and take a bite.

"Yesterday I was talking to my neighbor about collecting cans for the shelter. I asked her if she could save hers for me. And she told me if they can't find homes for the dogs at the shelter, they put them to sleep!"

"Put them to sleep?" I repeat, frowning.

"You know, *kill* them."

I stop chewing on my fish stick. I feel like I want to throw up. My heart starts thump thump thumping. Just because I don't want Beauregard doesn't mean I want him dead. This is horrible!

"He'll probably find a home." Grace touches my arm, trying to reassure me.

"But what if he doesn't?" I ask. "I mean, Saint

Bernards are big dogs. They drool. Maybe no one will want him." My throat tightens, and my eyes get all watery.

"What are you going to do?" Luanne asks.

"I've got to go back to the shelter. I have to tell the truth and get him back."

Grace, Luanne, and I walk down the sidewalk without hardly saying a word. Like we're on our way to a funeral. Or more likely to prevent one. Beauregard's. I can't believe the mess I've made of things.

Grace and Luanne are coming along for support. Grace told her mother, when she came to pick her up at school, that we had a group project to work on and asked if it was okay if we walked to the library together. The library is about two blocks away from school. And one block away from the library are Fenton Street and the shelter. So at least we will be in the general area. Her mother gave her permission, said she'd pick her up at the library in an hour and a half, and allowed Luanne and me to call our own mothers on her cell phone.

The sun is shining, and it has warmed up as the day has gone on—about sixty degrees and pleasant. But I feel all gloomy and rainy inside.

We get to the shelter, and there is the same woman at the front desk, Kathleen. She seems surprised to see me. "Well, hello again," she says.

"Hello. I was ah . . . wondering . . . ah . . . I heard . . ." I stumble around for the right words.

"Do you put dogs to sleep?" Luanne blurts out.

"'Cause we're real worried about that big dog," Grace adds.

I'm about to say, "'Cause he's mine," but the lady cuts me off before I can get the words out.

"Oh, we don't do that here. We're a small shelter and nowhere near capacity anyway. Some shelters do that because there isn't room for all the dogs that come in, but we don't have that problem yet. With luck we never will."

"What if Beau—if the dog I brought in doesn't find a home, though? How long will you keep him here?" I can't help thinking that living out the rest of his life in a cage at the shelter doesn't seem much better than the life my family's given him. Everything seemed so simple when I first thought of bringing him here. Now I'm not so sure.

Kathleen waves her hand in the air. "Oh, a dog like that one you don't have to worry about. I've already contacted a breed rescue group, since I'm positive he's a purebred Saint Bernard."

"What's a breed rescue group?" I ask.

"People who know and love and are experienced with certain breeds of dogs will come and get them from shelters," Kathleen says. "Then they find foster homes for them until a good permanent home can be found. The dogs are placed all over the country, so the dog you brought in might actually end up pretty far away from here, but he'll be well cared for."

Hearing those words made me feel I had done the right thing after all. Beauregard was in great hands. Everything was working out for the best.

"Well, then, I guess I won't worry about that dog I found," I say.

Or, I think, with relief, about Mama and Daddy finding out what I have done!

Chapter 12

Mama hovers over a pot of chili on the stove, while Daddy stands beside her, holding Justin Lee and complaining like crazy about the dognappers.

"There are dog thief rings, I heard. Killer's probably already for sale across state lines. No way to get him back. Makes me so mad I could spit," Daddy says.

I'm busy setting drinking cups around the table. And even though I'm happy for Beauregard and his future, I feel a little uneasy about the conversation. Guilty all of a sudden for keeping a secret from Mama and Daddy.

Justin Lee's face suddenly goes red, and he's straining.

"Uh-oh, I know what you're up to," Daddy says. "Want me to change him?" he asks Mama.

"Please," she replies.

Daddy disappears with his stinky son.

Mama dips a spoon into the chili, tasting it. She shakes some more pepper into the pot. "I don't think there were any dognappers," she whispers without looking at me.

I drop a plastic cup, and it rattles around on the linoleum floor. "You don't?" I ask, panicking. Maybe, from the upstairs window, she saw me take Beauregard.

"I think he probably just broke free somehow. He's a big dog. Strong."

"Oh."

"There's a new animal shelter in town—not sure Daddy knows about it yet. Someone could have found Killer roaming loose and took him there. I know you don't like taking care of that dog, and I'm tired of buying dog food, so don't mention it to Daddy. It's hard enough to work disposable diapers into the budget." Mama glances into the breezeway at her unfinished flower painting, which looks mostly like Justin Lee got into the paints, and makes a face. "Not to mention Daddy's bargain hunting habit," she says. She gives a half grin, like she realizes she just made a joke at Daddy's expense. And I realize I have had my first real conversation with her in a long time. Maybe she is starting to feel better.

"I won't say anything to Daddy," I tell her.

One more day, I think, and those dog rescue people can come pick up Beauregard. Then he'll probably end up clear across the country, and I won't have to worry about this whole business anymore. And maybe things will go back to normal.

Chapter 13

When I get home from school, I find a note on the fridge door. Mama is on an emergency run to the store for more diapers and says she'll be back soon. I open the fridge door and grab a can of grape soda. I'm about to head up to my room when I hear a deep bark.

A familiar bark.

I rush to the breezeway door and look out. And there is Beauregard. He sees me through the screen and barks again, his tail wagging a mile a minute.

I can't believe it.

I place my can of soda on a cluttered shelf and run outside. Beauregard acts like he hasn't seen me for years. He's so excited to see me he keeps jumping up and pulling at his chain. He wants me to pet him so badly he can hardly stand it. So I do. But I'm so much in shock I don't know what to think or feel.

I hear Mama's car pull in. I race around to the front of the house and find her unbuckling Justin Lee from his car seat.

"Killer's back," I say, breathless.

"I know," Mama says.

"How'd that happen?"

"Your daddy was still upset this morning about his supposedly being taken from our property. So he called the police to file a report. Then the police had to go call the animal shelter. Killer was there. Someone found him roaming around town and turned him in. So the police let Daddy know, and he went and picked him up during his lunch hour."

I try to take this all in. But I'm still in disbelief. Mama asks me to carry in the diapers, and I follow her and Justin Lee into the house.

Daddy's still convinced Beauregard was stolen.

"Killer must have gotten away from those dog thieves. Probably bolted and pulled loose before they could get him into the getaway car," he says during dinner.

I don't tell him any different, just nod my head in agreement.

"I didn't realize Greater Oaks got a new animal shelter. Did you?" Daddy asks Mama.

Mama just shrugs and says nothing. She sneaks a sideways glance at me, and her mouth twitches.

I told Grace and Luanne all about Beauregard's return at lunch, and now we're standing near the monkey bars, talking, during recess.

"You don't seem too upset about this," Luanne says.

"Yeah, and you were so close to getting Beauregard a new home," Grace adds.

I shrug. "You know what my daddy did last night? He went out and played with Beauregard for a half hour straight. He fed him and watered him this morning before eating his own breakfast, too. I think he is so glad to have him back that he's going to take better care of him."

I grin because in a weird way things may have just worked out after all for Beauregard and me.

Chapter 14

Next morning I wait and wait for Daddy to feed Beauregard. But he seems deep in thought over something, squinting at his cup of black coffee, so I go out and do it. Just like old times.

And when I return from school, Beauregard's water bowl is empty. I come back sloshing water and give him his belly rub after he's done quenching his thirst. We do a couple of rounds of "Shake"; he seems so proud he can shake hands, like he knows he's being smart somehow.

"Well, we're back to the drawing board again," I say. "Maybe you should be the one who comes up with the next plan since you're such a smarty-pants. Mine haven't been too successful."

That night I'm clearing the table of dirty dishes, since it's my week for that chore, and I'm listening to Mama and Daddy as they sit and talk at the table. Agnes is on the phone with her boyfriend, Tom. They are back together now. I hear her singsong voice chirping in the background.

Last night Daddy was still yapping about those dognappers, even though Beauregard had been returned safe and sound. Tonight he seems worried about something else.

"This morning I was thinkin' about how Killer let a stranger into our yard. And he let whoever it was take him right out from under our noses." Daddy pushes his chair back. "He didn't make a peep. He should have raised a ruckus. Should have barked his head off. I'm afraid he's not much of a watchdog." He shakes his head. "Maybe I ought to sell him. He's a nice dog, but he's not earning his keep."

Mama gets up and lifts Justin Lee out of his high chair. "That would be perfectly fine with me."

"I could sell him easy for maybe three or four hundred dollars."

"Call the paper and put an ad in," Mama says.

"I just might do that." Daddy nods.

I get busy, rinsing the dishes I have just cleared off the table. I look out the window above the sink at Beauregard. Hard to believe, but Daddy has come around to what I've wanted all along. Beauregard is going to get a new home, and I didn't even have to come up with a new scheme to make it happen.

I yawn. My emotions this week have been bobbing like a yo-yo, and it's making me feel all dizzy and worn-out.

I zonk right off to sleep, just about as soon as my head hits the pillow. But I wake up at three in the morning with a sick feeling in the pit of my stomach. I had a dream, one I don't have to struggle to try to remember. Why is it the good dreams always seem so fuzzy, and you have to reach back and fight to retrieve them, while the bad ones stick to you like superglue?

Daddy sold Beauregard in this dream. But there was no yellow kitchen. No plaid doggy bed. No painted dog bowls printed with his name. Only a chain. And a life worse than what he has now, 'cause there was no one like me to feel sorry for him. Beauregard was skin and bones in my dream, a skeleton with Saint Bernard skin, and someone was screaming at him. Even though I wasn't actually present in the dream myself—it wasn't like I was standing next to him or anything—he was still somehow able to stare at me with the most haunting eyes.

What if this dream comes true? Suddenly I remember a television show I watched a long time ago at Luanne's house. It was about animal cops, and they investigated a dog that was abused. Her owner kicked her, and she had a broken rib. How am I going to make sure Beauregard gets sold to someone who will treat him right?

Chapter 15

Despite not having a restful night's sleep, I wake up early on Friday morning, before I usually do, and find Daddy standing in front of the bathroom mirror, shaving.

I stand in the doorway, still in my nightgown. "If you sell Killer, how are we going to make sure he ends up in a good home?"

Daddy's razor pauses its up-and-down scratching motion.

"Why wouldn't he end up in a good home? I don't think it's anything to worry about."

"Some people are mean."

"Most aren't."

"But what if—"

Agnes staggers out of her room. "You almost done, Daddy? I need to take my shower."

"Almost. Listen, Charlotte, I'll just go with my gut instincts. I'm pretty good at reading people. I have a fifth sense about those things."

"You mean sixth sense, Daddy," Agnes says, rolling her eyes.

"That's it." Daddy takes one more swipe and rinses the foam from his face.

I start to say something, but Agnes interrupts me again. "Mama's still coming tonight to the home-coming game, isn't she?"

Daddy grabs a hand towel and pats his chin. "Of course. Why wouldn't she?" He stares at Agnes for a moment.

"'Cause she—" Agnes catches herself and gives me a quick look.

We aren't supposed to know anything is wrong.

"'Cause I heard the weather might be bad."

"That wouldn't stop her. Tonight's your big night; she'll be there."

Daddy smiles and walks out of the bathroom while Agnes rushes in, reassured by what he has just said about Mama. But I'm not reassured at all by what Daddy said about Beauregard. I don't quite trust that he can tell a good home from a bad one for Beauregard.

I head for the downstairs half bath since Agnes will be awhile, I'm sure.

That night Agnes comes swooping down the stairs in her new blue dress. She visited Rhonda's Cut and Curl after school today, and her hair is all fluffed out and sprayed stiff. Mama has some makeup on, the first time I've seen any on her in months, and she's putting on her good wool coat. She looks like the mama I remember. Even Daddy looks spiffed up with a nice flannel shirt on and dark jeans.

"Are you sure you're going to be okay?" Mama asks me.

I nod, shifting Justin Lee on my hip.

Tonight is my first baby-sitting job. I'll be taking care of Justin Lee while Mama and Daddy watch

Agnes as she sits with the queen's court at the home-coming game.

Originally we were all going to go, but it started to drizzle and the temperature fell to the low forties, so Mama didn't think it would be healthy for Justin Lee to be outside in the bad weather. I'm sort of sorry to be missing Agnes's big night, especially since Luanne and Grace were planning on going to the game too, but I'm glad to be helping Mama so she can go out and maybe have a good time.

"Mrs. Strickland next door is home if you need her. And Daddy's got the cell phone if you have any questions. Okay?" Mama looks a little worried.

Agnes rolls her eyes when the cell phone is mentioned. It's a sore subject with her. We have only one cell phone in the family, which we all share; whoever needs it the most gets it, and that's usually Daddy. Agnes thinks it's truly awful. She's been begging for one of her own. But Daddy says she has to wait until she starts driving. Then he'll get her one.

"Okay?" Mama says again, staring me down.

"Okay," I reply.

"She'll be fine," Daddy says, giving me a wink. He puts his arm around Mama, dwarfing her. "Charlotte will be twelve next week; that's the same age Agnes was when she started baby-sitting some of the neighbor kids."

"I know . . . ," Mama's voice trails off. She frowns at me, and I can tell she's worried since this will be my first time baby-sitting.

Mama, Daddy, and Agnes start walking toward the front door.

"Hope you have fun, Agnes," I say. "You look real nice."

Agnes gingerly touches her stiff hair and smiles at me. "Thanks."

"Lock up after us," Mama tells me.

"I will."

After locking the door, I look at Justin Lee, and he looks at me. Now what? I think. Mama has already given him his bath and fed him, and it's another hour until his bedtime.

Justin Lee grins at me. I grin back. He says some gobbledygook. I gobbledygook back at him. He starts to get heavy, so I put him down. Then he crawls over to a basket of baby toys Mama keeps next to the television set. I get out a plastic mailbox with plastic letters, and he gets busy putting the colorful rect-angles into a slot. When he gets tired of that, I grab some board books and read to him on the couch. He pats the thick pages and slobbers and sputters some sounds out. I haven't a clue what he is saying, but by his expression he seems to think he is quite eloquent. I look at the clock on the wall. Only ten minutes have passed since Mama, Daddy, and Agnes left. I sigh.

Justin Lee sighs, copying me, and he's got the most serious look on his face.

I start laughing. Then he starts laughing. We're sharing a moment, Justin Lee and me. Just when I think this might actually be kind of fun, my brother starts wailing. I have no idea what has upset him. Mama has three of his pacifiers lined up on the coffee table, so I grab one and stick it in his mouth. This quiets him down. We visit the toy basket again, read some more books, have a few more laughs, a few more crying spells, and finally, after what seems like an eternity, I am able to tuck him into his crib upstairs. No wonder Mama seems so tired all the time! I'm exhausted. But I'm proud of myself, too. I think I've done a good job for my first time baby-sitting.

I go downstairs and flop on the couch. Flip through some channels, but nothing looks interesting. I think about reading a book I checked out at the library. I'm on the third chapter, but I'm having a hard time getting into it, and it doesn't seem worth the trip upstairs to fetch it. So I find a small note-pad used for writing down telephone messages and doodle for a while on it. I draw funny faces, a pretty princess, and a hairy monster with sharp teeth. I wish I had a nice big sketchbook, but I usually make do with whatever scraps of paper I can find. After I fill up a few pages, I try to think of something else to occupy the remaining time.

Over in the corner is a desk set up with our family computer, another one of Daddy's bargains. A couple of years ago his boss upgraded and sold his old computer to Daddy for a hundred dollars. There's an arcade site that I sometimes log on to that has some fun games. But once I get situated in front of the screen, I notice it isn't drizzling outside anymore. It's pouring down rain. I know it's cold outside, too. But instead of feeling bad about Agnes's new hairdo flattening out as she sits, shivering, under an umbrella, in a metal folding chair on the sidelines with the other homecoming royalty, I think of Beauregard.

I run to the breezeway and look out. There he is, stuffed as well as he can be into his too small doghouse. Even though it's dark, I can see the shadow of his big head sticking out. He's resting it on his paws, as the rain pelts down.

If only I could find something to shelter him a bit better. I glance around the breezeway and notice Daddy's painting sitting on its windowsill easel. Daddy started painting again after the excitement of Beauregard being missing, then found. It's about halfway done now and taking shape. You can actually tell it's a bouquet of flowers in a vase and not just swirls on top of a yellow blob. Maybe I got my artistic talent from him. Who'd have thought? Next to the painting stuff I find a big plastic storage container where Mama keeps rolls of wrapping paper, ribbons, and tissue paper. I pop the lid off and run outside with it.

In a few seconds I'm drenched, but I prop the lid against the front of the doghouse and it makes a little roof for Beauregard. I'd ask Daddy to at least make him a new doghouse that fits, but with Daddy talking yesterday about selling him, I know he wouldn't bother.

After drying off and changing into a cozy pair of pajamas, I go back and sit in front of the computer again. But instead of logging on to the arcade site, I bring up Google.

Then, for some reason, even though I know it won't help, I type in "Saint Bernard Breed Rescue."

Chapter 16

I click on saintrescue.org. At the top of the page is a logo of a cute little girl with an armband and stethoscope listening to a Saint Bernard's heart. Near the logo it says in big red letters "Saint Bernard Rescue Foundation, Inc."

I pull up the adoption form people can fill out if they want a Saint Bernard. It asks what other dogs you have and if the dogs are up-to-date on their shots. How many adults and children are in the family and who will be caring for the adopted dog. If anyone has allergies and how many hours the dog might be left alone during the day. Where the dog will sleep and if a fenced-in yard will be provided and, if so, a description of the fence. It asks if you will agree to a home check and if you would be willing to housebreak the dog. The questions go on and on. They seem to really want to make sure the dog will go to a good home.

I sigh, wishing Daddy had never called the police when Beauregard went missing. There is no way Daddy will be as thorough when it comes to checking out prospective owners. Not when he thinks he can depend on his "fifth" sense. I mean, what is he going to do, sniff the people coming to buy Beauregard? I laugh at that image, despite being worried. Maybe tomorrow, though, I can suggest to Daddy some of the requirements the Saint Bernard rescue group uses. He can put them in his ad.

I look at the listings for last year and am amazed to find out 591 dogs were rescued and adopted out last year. This group found homes for 591 dogs just like Beauregard! Each dog has a picture, description, and date adopted. I spend a while studying each listing, then settle in and read adoption stories, where new owners write in to tell how they are doing.

There's Hercules, who didn't look like a Hercules at all at first, according to the person who adopted him. He was skinny, fifty pounds underweight. But with love, care, and a good appetite, he grew strong, and finally his name fit. In fact the woman who adopted him developed health problems—she had trouble with balance and getting up—so she took him to mobility training, and he became her therapy dog.

Then there was Matilda. A breeder no longer had any use for her, so she was transported from Florida all the way to a new home in Alaska, of all places. And Hank, whose owner reports his favorite place to go is Dairy Queen; he is especially fond of butterscotch sundaes. And Reba, who visits a nursing home every week with her owner and causes traffic jams in the hallways 'cause all the residents are so glad to see her. And Jezebel, who thinks she is a tiny little lapdog; her owner has to warn people who visit about the possibility of 230 pounds of love smothering them once they sit down. I get lost in the stories of happy owners and pictures of their happy dogs. There are Saint Bernards pictured reclining on comfy couches, Saint Bernards with kids climbing on them, Saint Bernards with big rawhide bones or prized balls in their mouths.

Suddenly there is the sound of keys in the front door. I quickly close the saintrescue.org window and jump up.

As soon as Mama steps in, she asks how things went.

"Fine. Justin Lee was good, and he went right off to sleep."

Daddy shakes off his umbrella before stepping inside. "Holy cow, it was miserable out there."

Agnes follows him in, looking upset. Her hair is an odd combination of frizzy and flat. "Of all the nights to rain." She frowns.

"Aw, you looked mighty pretty down there anyway," Daddy says, trying to cheer her up.

"I don't think anyone could see me at all through the rain. But it's just as well; I probably looked like a drowned rat. They should have canceled the game."

"No lightning or thunder. Rules say you gotta play, sweetheart," Daddy tells her.

"Well, they should have made an exception for homecoming."

All three of them look wet from the knees down, where an umbrella couldn't protect them, and they kick off soggy shoes. An hour from now they will be dry and snug under the covers, though.

I think how if it weren't for me, Beauregard would have had raindrops falling on his head all night long. Still, a propped-up plastic container top doesn't exactly take care of all his problems. I think of all the lucky dogs adopted through the Saint Bernard rescue group. None of them having to be left out in the rain.

"I'm going to go upstairs to check on Justin Lee," Mama says.

"Oh, he's okay. Charlotte took good care of him," Daddy says, ruffling my hair. "Besides, honey, you might wake him if you go into his room."

Mama shakes her head and trudges up the stairs. "He'll be awake and crying in a few hours anyway."

Entertaining Justin Lee was hard enough for the short time I cared for him. I can't imagine being responsible for him all the time. No wonder Mama's running shoes stay in the closet!

Chapter 17

Next morning Mama is shoving spoonfuls of oatmeal into Justin Lee's mouth. He has mastered finger food but can't handle a spoon yet. Mama has a grin on her face, and she is humming.

I grab a cereal box out of the cabinet and wonder why she is in such a good mood. I don't have to wonder long, though.

"Guess what?" she says.

"What?"

"Justin Lee slept through the night! Whatever you did last night, when you were baby-sitting, must have worked some magic on him. What did you do? Let him crawl up the stairs a million times so he got all tuckered out?" Mama asked.

"Nope. Just read to him, and he played with his toys in the basket. That's all."

Mama puts down the spoon, wipes a glob of oatmeal off Justin Lee's face with a napkin, and picks up the spoon again.

Justin Lee grabs the spoon away from Mama and pounds his high chair tray with it.

Mama looks at me. "I really hope this isn't just a fluke and that he sleeps through the night from now on."

I pour my cereal into a bowl and sit down with Mama and Justin Lee.

The phone rings, and Mama asks me to get it, as she is busy trying to wrangle the spoon back from Justin Lee. His bowl of oatmeal still has a bit left in the bottom, and Mama's determined that he finish it.

I dash over to the phone. "Hello?"

A gruff voice greets me; the returned "hello" through the receiver kind of reminds me of Darth

Vader. There're a few raspy breaths; then whoever it is says, "I'm calling about the Saint Bernard for sale."

Oh, Lord. Daddy must have already put an ad in the paper. He just mentioned it two days ago! I thought I'd have more time to talk things over with him.

There's another raspy breath. No way I'm letting someone who sounds like Darth Vader buy Beauregard.

"You must have the wrong phone number," I say.

There is an abrupt "sorry," then a click.

I hang up the phone.

"What was that about?" Mama asks.

I shrug. "Some guy asking for someone named Mary." I say a silent prayer Darth Vader doesn't call back.

The *Greater Oaks Record* is lying on the kitchen table. I busy myself with reading the funnies until Mama and Justin Lee leave the room. Then I flip through the pages until I find the classifieds. I follow my finger up and down through columns of tiny print until I come across the pet section. And there it is. Daddy's ad. It simply says: "Saint Bernard $350.00 or best offer." Underneath it is an ad for a golden retriever. It says: "Great disposition, loves children, needs a large yard, good home only, references required." I close the paper wishing Daddy would have at least mentioned "good home only" just like the other ad. "Or best offer" sounds like he is trying to sell a car. Who knows who else will be calling besides Darth Vader? Maybe the Wicked Witch of the West; she wasn't exactly kind to Toto.

I spend the next hour hanging out in the kitchen by myself. It's boring just sitting at the table—I finished my cereal long ago and every article in the paper, too—but I want to reach the phone before anyone else can, just in case it happens to ring again. But there has been nothing but silence.

I find a pencil in our kitchen junk drawer so I can draw on the borders of the comic page. I sit back at the table and create little pictures of Snoopy, Beetle Bailey, Garfield, and Hagar the Horrible. Soon there is no white space left. I begin wondering if I should run upstairs to grab my library book, even though I can't seem to get past the third chapter. At least it would be more interesting than the city council meeting notes I read earlier. I'm desperate for anything to pass the time—

A shrill sound makes me nearly jump out of my skin.

The phone. I stumble to my feet and make a mad dash for it, but Agnes whips around the corner, out of nowhere, and grabs it before me.

"Hello?" she says, all breathless and hopeful.

I'm standing next to her, staring, my heart pounding.

She frowns at me and cups her hand over the receiver. "It's Tom," she says. "Go away."

I figure she will be on the phone for a while, so I slip upstairs for my book.

After Agnes finally finishes talking to her true love (at least for the moment), I settle in at the kitchen table, open my book, and before long I finally get sucked into the story. It's turning out to be a good book after all. Maddie, the main character, who is selfish and has always had servants taking care of her, has become lost in the woods. It's starting to get cold and dark. She's hungry. And she needs to use the bathroom—

Uh-oh, I suddenly realize I need to use the bathroom, too.

I stare at the phone and try to wait it out, but after ten minutes I can't stand it. I bolt for the downstairs half bath, and the second I'm sitting on the toilet with my jeans below my knees the phone rings. I mutter a word my mama wouldn't approve of and jump up, pulling my jeans back to my waist. I fling the door open, but it's too late. I hear Daddy's voice booming "hello."

Chapter 18

"Yes," I hear Daddy say, "he's a purebred. I have his AKC papers."

I run full speed over to him, never minding my still-full bladder, and tug on his sleeve. "Daddy," I blurt out, "there's already a buyer for Killer."

Daddy's eyebrows shoot up. "There is?"

I nod.

Daddy tells the person on the line, "Excuse me for a minute." He cups his hand over the receiver. "How much are they going to pay for him?" he asks.

"Four hundred dollars," I say—more than the ad asked for.

Daddy frowns for a moment in thought. Finally he takes his hand off the receiver. "I've already got an offer of four hundred for him. Would you be willing to top that?" There is a pause. Then Daddy says, "Oh, I see." He hangs up the phone. "A breeder from West Townfield," he tells me. "She was only willing to pay three hundred for him. Now, who's buying my dog?"

I stare at my feet and bite my lip.

"Who's buying the dog, Charlotte?"

I dare a peek at Daddy. He's got his hands on his hips, and he's staring at me like he's all of a sudden afraid I'm up to no good.

"Uh . . . I am?" The words just pop out, but as soon as they're said, I realize maybe I have accidentally stumbled onto a brilliant solution.

Daddy's red face grows redder. "I just lost a sale because of you. Didn't even get the woman's number, so I can't call her back." I can tell Daddy is real mad, but then he does what he always does when me or Agnes gets in trouble: he yells for Mama.

She comes into the kitchen, looking annoyed. She's got Justin Lee in her arms, and he's fussing over something; his face is all scrunched up, and he's making growling noises. It's pretty obvious she isn't too happy either; not only does she have to deal with a grumpy baby, but an unhappy husband as well. "What?" she says.

"I had someone interested in Killer, and Charlotte went and ruined it for me."

"Mama." I cross my legs. "I really have to use the bathroom. Could you please punish me after I'm done?"

Daddy sees my crossed legs, and he can't help himself. He starts laughing.

Justin Lee struggles to be put down, and Mama stands him on the floor, clasping his hands. "Go do your business first," Mama says.

"Thanks." I uncross my legs, and then something incredible happens. Justin Lee shakes his hands free of Mama's and takes five wobbly steps over to me.

"Char Char," he says, grinning, reaching up.

I forget my uncomfortable bladder for a moment and scoop him up.

Mama's hand flies up to her mouth. "His first steps

and his first word," she gasps. "And he just turned ten months old!"

"Put him down; see if he'll walk to me," Daddy says. He kneels, stretching out his arms. "Come on, buddy!"

I place Justin Lee's feet on the floor, and he stumbles toward Daddy like he's had one too many, but he doesn't fall and makes it safely to his outstretched arms. Daddy picks him up and twirls him around. "That's my boy!"

While Mama's busy clapping, I make a beeline to the bathroom.

Chapter 19

We are all seated in the living room, Daddy and Mama on the couch and me in the chair across from them. Justin Lee partly crawled, partly walked over to the basket, got out one of his board books, and brought it back to me. Now he's snuggled in my lap, and I'm using him as a shield of sorts. Mama and Daddy are looking at me, but since their one and only son just took his first steps a few minutes ago, the proud expressions on their faces do a good job of masking whatever anger they might have at me.

I give Justin Lee a gentle squeeze. I owe him. Big time.

"Why?" Mama finally asks. "Why did you lie to your father?"

"I didn't really." While relieving myself in the bathroom, I finalized my hastily come-up-with plan. "Listen, that woman wasn't going to pay Daddy what he wants for Killer. And I'm going to pay Daddy four hundred dollars for him."

"For crying out loud, Charlotte, weren't you the one who wanted me to get rid of Killer? Just last month you were pestering me to give him away. This isn't making any sense!" Daddy growls at me.

"Not to mention you don't have four hundred dollars anyway," Mama says.

"Well, see, I guess I suddenly realized how attached I've gotten to Killer." I lie. "I just can't bear to see him go." I sniff like I'm about to cry. "Mama, you haven't gotten my birthday present yet, have you?"

"Not yet. But I certainly wasn't going to spend four hundred dollars on you!"

"I know, but whatever you were planning to spend you could apply toward the four hundred. Couldn't you?" I wipe away an imaginary tear.

"Honey, that would only be about forty dollars," Mama says.

"But Grandma June and Grandpa Harry always send a card with a twenty in it. And Aunt Renee always gives me fifteen."

Daddy adds the numbers up. "So that's seventy-five dollars. You'd still have a balance then of three hundred twenty-five. Where's that coming from, may I ask?"

"I'll get a job."

Daddy snorts, then grins. "You're only eleven years old!"

"I'll be twelve next week," I tell him.

Justin Lee takes the board book and, tired of waiting for me to read it, thumps me on the head with it. "Char Char," he says.

"I did a good job of baby-sitting for Justin Lee," I tell Mama. "He slept through the night, and now he's walking and talking."

"It's truly astounding. But I think Justin Lee deserves most of the credit," Mama says. "He was just ready."

"But I did do a good job baby-sitting him," I say.

"Yes, you did." Mama nods.

"So I was thinking, maybe I could watch Justin Lee for you on a regular basis. That could be my job, and you could get a break from him and maybe get some things done or go somewhere."

"Charlotte, I can't afford to pay you on a regular basis. Besides, he's your brother, and I shouldn't have to pay you at all. It's called being a part of the family and helping out."

"Oh." I didn't think that was quite fair, but I didn't want to start an argument with Beauregard's welfare at stake. I was already in enough trouble as it was. "Well, I'll find something else to do to earn the money. I promise I will." I take the book from Justin Lee, open it, and start reading to him, acting like I'm finally in the clear. "Ball," I say, pointing to the picture.

"How long should we give her?" Mama asks.

"Three months. Not a day more," Daddy says. "Miss Charlotte?"

I look up from the book about balls, bears, bees, and other *B* words.

"You have three months to pay me my four hundred dollars. Today's October ninth. If I don't have the money in full by January ninth, I will put another ad in the paper and sell Killer."

"Okay." I point at a new picture in the book. "Baby," I say. "Just like you!" I poke Justin Lee in his chubby little tummy. I think about asking Mama and Daddy not to get me a Christmas gift either, but it would seem a little sad not having something to open up on Christmas morning. Since I already gave up a birthday gift, I don't mention it. I'm sacrificing enough for that dog. I figure I should already have Beauregard paid off by then anyway.

"She must really love that dog if she's willing to pay four hundred dollars to keep him," Daddy tells Mama.

"Well, after she's done paying for him, she should be responsible for buying his bags of dog food, too." Mama says.

"If I can come up with the four hundred dollars, I should be able to come up with the money to feed him, too." I don't move my eyes from the book.

"Blanket," I say. This time Justin Lee points to the picture. I think he tries to say the word *blanket*, but it doesn't sound like it at all.

Of course I don't want to keep Beauregard. After he's paid in full, I'm going to give him to the rescue group I read about on the Internet. I figure I'll just let Mama and Daddy know all the details when the time comes. If I tell them now, they might change their minds about the whole thing. I have a feeling Daddy might get insulted with the idea that Beauregard needs to be rescued from our home.

Chapter 20

I don't waste any time. As soon as I'm done reading Justin Lee his *B* book, I head next door to Mrs. Strickland's. She's a nurse, and her husband's in the army. He's stationed overseas right now and won't be back until spring, so I figure she might need some help raking leaves this fall. She has a couple of big old trees in her front yard, and a few leaves have already started to drift down. Then this winter I could offer to shovel her sidewalks and driveway.

I ring the doorbell and wait a few moments, trying to rehearse what I should say; I need to sound mature and professional, after all, if I expect to get paid for a job. I get it sounding right in my head, but no one opens the door. Maybe she is at work? Just as I start to trot down the steps, I hear the door open behind me.

"Hi, Charlotte. You caught me taking cookies out of the oven. Sorry I didn't get to the door sooner."

"That's okay. I'm trying to earn money for a—a special project. And I was wondering if maybe I could rake leaves this fall and then shovel snow this winter for you."

Mrs. Strickland steps out onto the porch. "Sweetie, I'm sorry. Dustin Greenfield from down the street is already lined up to do that for me. And before you go door to door asking anyone else, it seems he has pretty much captured the market for raking and shoveling in this neighborhood. He gave me a list of references; I guess he's been doing it for a few years now."

"Oh." I can feel my face sinking in disappointment. Dustin Greenfield is a high school kid, the same age as Agnes. He lives about four doors down. Even though he seems perfectly nice, I sense a grudge coming on. Next time he zips by my house on his bike, you won't catch me waving to him. And he zips by our house quite often. I think he has a bit of a crush on Agnes.

Mrs. Strickland, in an effort to cheer me up, asks if I want a warm, freshly baked chocolate chip cookie.

Even though it doesn't make up for the lost job opportunity, I go ahead and say, "Sure."

Munching on the warm cookie Mrs. Strickland has given me, which I have to admit is delicious, I make the short trip to my own backyard to check on Beauregard's water bowl. It's half full.

Beauregard eyes the half-eaten cookie in my hand like it is the most interesting thing he has ever seen. I crack off a piece that doesn't have melted chocolate oozing out (I remember Luanne saying that dogs are allergic to chocolate) and extend it toward him. Just like with the gingersnaps, instead of lunging for it and snapping it away, Beauregard daintily gathers it into his mouth. Then he licks his lips and stares a thank-you at me.

I laugh, pat his head, stuff the rest of the cookie

into my mouth, then trudge off to fill up his water bowl. He is such a gentle giant with perfect manners. Whoever gets him from Saint Bernard rescue will be very lucky. But I've got to find a job first. Struck out with paid baby-sitting. Struck out with raking leaves and shoveling snow, thanks to Dustin Greenfield. What else can an almost twelve-year-old do?

I decide to go over to Luanne's house. Maybe she will come up with something.

"Why don't you baby-sit kids other than Justin Lee?" Luanne asks after I explain what has happened. The two of us are sitting on her bed, and Luanne's holding a sleeping Jester in her lap. His legs twitch in dreamland, and his mouth is clamped around his yellow stuffed duck toy.

"Everyone already calls Agnes if they need a sitter," I say. "She's been doing it for two years now, so she's got the market all wrapped up."

"How about cocktail waitress?" Luanne says, grabbing a purple ruffled pillow and throwing it at me. "You get good tips."

I let the pillow hit me in the head, and it bounces to the floor. Jester stretches and yawns, dropping the doggy toy from his mouth.

"Get serious." I lean over and rest my chin in my hand. "If I can't come up with the money in time, he might end up in a worse situation than he has now. He could be abused, not just neglected. I can't stand the thought of that happening."

"Okay." Luanne squints in thought and taps her fingers to her cheek. "Hmm . . ."

Before she can come up with anything, her mom enters the room. When I saw her earlier, she was wearing jeans and a T-shirt. But now she has on a snug long black skirt and a lime green blouse.

"You look nice, Mom," Luanne says.

I nod in agreement. Luanne has a really pretty mom anyway, but right now she looks like a movie star.

"Mom and Dad's anniversary is today." Luanne explains the reason for her mom being all dolled up. "They are going to drop me off with my grandparents; I'm spending the night so they can have a rooooomantic dinner and evening together."

Mrs. Beckler smiles and rolls her eyes.

"Maybe now would be a good time to mention that baby sister I want," Luanne whispers to me, but loud enough for her mother to hear.

Mrs. Beckler blushes and shakes her head. "Luanne!" She turns her attention to me. "I love what you did to Luanne's hair the other day—the French braid. Do you think you could fix my hair like that, too? It's not lying right, and I'm tired of messing with it."

"Sure."

Minutes later Mrs. Beckler is sitting in a kitchen chair, and I'm behind her, strips of dark hair between my fingers, twisting and weaving. And right when I'm not thinking about jobs and making money, an idea pops into my head.

Chapter 21

Monday morning, after I've fed and taken care of Beauregard and am ready to head off to school, I realize I have forgotten something. Mrs. Delenor's class project. I'm supposed to bring items I've collected for the animal shelter to school today. Only I never did collect anything. I planned on spending time over the weekend gathering things, but after that phone call Saturday morning it totally left my mind.

I rush into the breezeway and find the collar Beauregard wore when Daddy first brought him home. He quickly outgrew it, and it got tossed in a pile with some other useless items. I then rummage through the kitchen trash can and find four pop cans. It's not much, but at least I'm not coming empty-handed.

When I get to school, I feel a little embarrassed. A lot of kids obviously spent a ton of time and put a great deal of thought into the community service assignment. Grace has a huge box containing five rolls of paper towels, a bag of cat litter, a small bag of dog food, and several new leashes with the price tags still hanging from silver clasps.

Luanne has two garbage bags full of pop cans; early on she went door to door, asking people to save their empty cans, and then on Sunday, when she got back from her grandparents', she and her dad went around and picked them all up. Some kids brought so much stuff they had to have help from their parents to carry it all into the classroom.

I'm glad we are not getting a grade for what we bring in!

We get out our social studies books, and Mrs. Delenor goes over the chapter six questions we had for homework. Finally, at ten o'clock, she tells us it is time to go on our field trip.

"Gary's father has offered the use of his truck to transport the items you've collected," she says.

Gary Blankenship is sitting next to me, and he sits up tall in his seat and smiles proudly. His father just got a brand-new red pickup truck, and he had been bragging about it all last week.

"And good thing he has volunteered. You all did such a great job with the service project there's no way we could carry everything you brought to the shelter!"

Well, I actually would have no problem carrying what I brought. . . .

It was spitting rain earlier this morning, but fortunately it has cleared up for our walk to the shelter. Gary's father drove ahead in his shiny red truck, once we got everything loaded, and is probably already there, waiting for us.

I'm walking right between Luanne and Grace, and I'm whispering to Grace about what happened over the weekend: how Daddy tried to sell Beauregard, but I stopped him, and how I need to earn $325 to buy him myself, so I can give him to the rescue group.

"She's come up with a great idea." Luanne leans forward to tell her. "But she needs our help."

"Do you think you can come over after school?" I ask.

"I think so," Grace says slowly. "Now that my mother has met your mother, and she really liked you when you came over, it will probably be okay. I'll ask her when she comes to pick me up."

"Good."

"But I don't understand, what do you need *my* help for?" Grace looks confused.

When I tell her, she thinks it's an excellent idea. Luanne thought it was an excellent idea when I told her, too, on Saturday. And I'm sure it won't be long at all until I'm handing over that $325 (plus my birthday money) to Daddy.

Everyone's got an armload of stuff, gathered from the back of Gary's father's truck, and we are met by Kathleen at the front door, the very Kathleen I brought Beauregard to a week ago in my foiled attempt to find him a decent home.

I suddenly get uncomfortable. I try to blend into the middle of the group of kids, while hiding my face behind the pile of shelter donations I'm carrying.

What if she recognizes me and says something about me bringing a Saint Bernard to the shelter? Some of my classmates, besides Luanne and Grace, know my family has a Saint Bernard. If they mention it, Kathleen might put two and two together. What if she asks if I brought in my own dog? Maybe she'd have to tell the police she found the dognapper, and then the police would tell my parents. I'd be in really big trouble. Maybe Mama and Daddy would be so mad they'd go back on their deal to let me buy Beauregard.

Kathleen leads us to their storage area, an old wooden garage type of structure in back of the shelter building. She grabs a handle and lifts up one of the wide doors and has us deposit the items inside, where an open space has been cleared. "I'll sort through everything later," she says. "Thank you so much!"

There's still stuff left in the back of Gary's father's truck, so Mrs. Delenor has us go back for a second trip to carry things to the garage. I grab a thirty-pound bag of dog food so it will cover me from the waist up. But soon all the donations are stacked up in the storage garage, and it's time for the tour. And I have nothing to hide behind. I decide my best bet is to stand behind everyone else.

First stop is the reception area and desk. Kathleen shows everyone an adoption form and explains the procedure and fees involved. Next is the cat room. Kids start asking questions, and Kathleen focuses her attention on those who have their hands raised. I start to breathe easier.

After that we go on to the room where new dogs are brought and kept for three days, the room Beauregard never made it out of because my daddy had to go and call the police about his "stolen" dog. There is only one dog in there now, a short-haired tan-and-white dog barking for attention. All the kids crowd around his kennel cage as Kathleen talks about having the dogs checked for health and behavior issues and how owners have three days to claim a dog that has been brought in. Since she is now behind the flock of kids, I don't feel safe in back of everyone, so I crowd my way into the middle of the group.

Unfortunately the next stop is the dog adoption room, and there are eight dogs occupying a row of cages. My classmates all spread out to visit with different dogs. Grace and Luanne go over to the far side of the room, where there is a small poodleish-looking dog. Kathleen is close to where we entered, standing near a few boys who are sticking their hands into a cage so they can pet a chocolate Lab. I join Grace and Luanne at the far end of the room and pretend to be interested in the tiny, curly-haired mop of a dog. Out of the corner of my eye I can see Kathleen slowly making her way down the row of dogs, getting closer and closer to where I am. She's stopping at each kennel to talk about each dog and answer questions.

I wonder if I should make my way over to the

chocolate Lab, where she has already been. But then I would have to pass her. I decide to remain with Grace and Luanne.

Before Kathleen has even made it down to where we are, I hear a "Hey, I know you girls!"

Grace and Luanne are nodding and grinning beside me. My face is frozen with panic.

Kathleen points at me. "You brought in a dog. And then you came back with your friends because you were worried about him. Well, guess what? His owner's been located!"

I try to look surprised by this news. She did not mention the breed of dog, thank goodness. So at least no one can make a comment about me bringing in the exact same type of dog my family has.

"Isn't that great? Now you won't have to worry about him anymore!" she says.

Oh, if she only knew . . .

Chapter 22

Mrs. Walters gives Grace permission to go to my house after school and is nice enough to give me, Grace, and Luanne a ride there. After being clear most of the day, it has started to rain again, so at least we won't have to face a wet walk home.

I asked Mama last night if Grace and Luanne could come over, so she's not surprised to see all of us tumbling through the front door. She stops folding a peach-colored towel long enough to tell me we are welcome to raid the snack cabinet in the kitchen. She actually smiles. Justin Lee slept through the night again.

Justin Lee squeals and shows off his newfound

talent to my friends: walking. He takes about six steps and then lands smack on his bottom.

"Hey, you didn't tell me he learned to walk," Luanne says. She claps for him. "What a big boy you are!"

Even though he fell, Justin Lee looks very proud of himself.

I lead Luanne and Grace into the kitchen, get them each a chocolate chip granola bar from the cabinet for an after-school snack, and excuse myself so I can tend to Beauregard. I grab a beige umbrella from the front hall closet and head out the breeze-way door. Since it rained earlier this morning and is raining again now, he really doesn't need his water bowl filled up, but he does expect a belly rub. I make a face and kneel, my hand sweeping over damp, dirty fur. I guess one bath doesn't mean he's clean forever.

"Won't be long," I tell him. "Just hang on for three more months, and you'll get as many belly rubs as you want and you'll be dry and warm when it's cold and cool and comfortable when it's hot. You'll have a real home to live in—not a chain and too small doghouse."

✺ ✺ ✺

Luanne, Grace, and I are walking down Fenton Street. Gray skies, but only a few little spits of water falling down now. Still, I make Luanne and Grace stay under the beige umbrella. I don't want the moisture ruining their hair. I French-braided Luanne's black hair just exactly as I did before. But I tried something different with Grace's hair. I divided the hair in half and made two French braids, one going down each side of her head. I walk behind them, so I can admire my handiwork, an occasional splat of water hitting my shoulders since I am umbrellaless.

Luanne leans in close to say something to Grace, and the side of her head brushes against the umbrella post.

"Careful!" I call out. I don't want a single stray hair escaping.

Finally we are all three standing in front of Rhonda's Cut and Curl. I open the door, which jingles, take the umbrella from Grace's hand, and usher my two friends in.

Rhonda is busy rolling some lady's short gray hair into tiny pink rollers. "Hey, Charlotte," she says, smiling. Another hairdresser I don't recognize is snipping scissors through Dustin Greenfield's mother's hair. Mrs. Greenfield waves to me. I decide, since I'm about to get a job, not to hold a grudge about her son's leaf raking and snow shoveling business, so I wave back.

It's been a while since I've had my hair trimmed up—about six months—and I notice that Rhonda has grown considerably since I saw her last. Well, at least her stomach has. She's pregnant. Very pregnant!

Rhonda says, "I don't remember your name on the books, Charlotte. You don't have an appointment, do you?"

I shake my head no. "I just need to talk to you. But I can wait till you're done."

Rhonda continues rolling up gray hair while Grace, Luanne, and I sit in the little waiting area. I try to busy myself by looking through some tattered hairstyle magazines.

Ten minutes later Rhonda puts the pink roller lady under a hair dryer and walks over to us.

"What can I do for you?" she asks. "Selling

something for the school? Candy? Magazines?"

"No." I motion for Grace and Luanne to get up. I spin them around so the backs of their heads are facing Rhonda. "I French-braid hair. I'd like to work here after school."

Rhonda seems a little startled by this news. It takes a moment for her to find her voice. "Charlotte, honey, your friends look lovely. They truly do. I couldn't do a better braid if I tried, really. But you have to go to school and get a license to work in a beauty shop if you want to do anything to another person's hair. I'm sorry."

Luanne and Grace drop their heads in disappointment for me. They slowly turn around. I want to burst out crying. I thought for sure I'd have a job here at Rhonda's Cut and Curl. I imagined five or six customers a day as news spread of my braiding skills. And money stuffed in my pockets.

A motion catches the corner of my eye. The other hairdresser is sweeping up clippings from Mrs. Greenfield's freshly cut hair.

"I could sweep!" I say. "I wouldn't need a license for that!"

Rhonda gets this concerned look in her eyes. "Are you having some sort of financial problems at home? Did your daddy get laid off? Or leave?"

Goodness, if I told her Daddy up and left us, she'd probably feel sorry for me and give me a job. But what an awful lie to tell. And finances are tight, but we aren't in dire straits. Besides, the last time I lied to the shelter lady about Beauregard being a stray, things didn't exactly turn out the way I planned.

As it so happens, I don't have to say a thing, though, 'cause Rhonda says real quicklike, "I guess it's none of my business what's going on in your house. That's private. But you do need to earn some money, don't you?"

I nod.

"Listen." She pats her big belly. "I'm due in a couple of weeks. Julie over there will be filling in for me here for a while. She's a friend of mine from West Townfield, and she just got her beautician's license. But every day at lunch, around one o'clock, I go over to check on my husband's great-aunt. She lives in that huge yellow Victorian across the street." Rhonda points out the window.

It's the house my mama has always admired. The one she would buy and fix up if she ever won the lottery.

"She's eighty-three and had a stroke a few years ago," Rhonda tells me. "Has trouble getting around, so I walk down the street to get her mail from the post office; she has a PO box there. I've been telling her to put a mailbox near her front door, but she's quite stubborn. Always had a PO box and doesn't want to change. I also run to the corner store—Grater's—to pick up a few groceries for her if she needs anything. Then I spend a little time visiting with her. Anyway, I live about twenty minutes outside town, so once my little bundle of joy comes along, it will be harder to check on her; it won't be as simple as just walking across the street. Maybe you could do that for me for six weeks or so? After school you could stop by for about an hour and make sure she has her mail and enough to eat and is okay. What do you think? I'd have to talk it over with her first, of course, but I'm thinking maybe she could pay you ten dollars a day. It will only be

Monday through Friday. My husband checks on her during the weekend."

I stand there dumbfounded. Did she just offer me a job?

Luanne nudges me. Grace is grinning like crazy.

"Sounds good," I say.

"Stop by here tomorrow after school, and I'll let you know if it's a done deal or not."

I quickly calculate the numbers in my head. Ten dollars a day, that would make fifty dollars a week. At six weeks, I'd make . . . three hundred dollars, most of what I need. And I'd have another six weeks or so left to somehow earn the remaining twenty-five.

The door jingles behind us as Grace, Luanne, and I leave Rhonda's Cut and Curl. Me and Beauregard are on easy street now!

I stop for a moment to stare at the big monster of a place across the way. Peeling green gingerbread trim frames much of the house, and even though the wood siding is a faded yellow, it doesn't exactly look cheerful. It has stopped raining altogether, but an unexpected bolt of lightning flashes from behind, making the place look like some sort of haunted house from a movie. I only hope the occupant isn't as scary-looking. An eighty-three-year-old who has suffered a stroke. What, I suddenly wonder, have I gotten myself into?

Chapter 23

I walk to Rhonda's Cut and Curl after school the next day, wondering if I have a job or not. Part of me is desperately hoping for the job, while part of me is desperately wishing Rhonda will say it won't work out. I'm a little scared of going into that creepy old house and looking after what could be a creepy old woman. I feel guilty for being uncomfortable that way; just because someone is old and has had a stroke doesn't mean she can't be nice, after all. But still, I can't shake the feeling things will be awkward.

Mama and Daddy have given me permission to accept Rhonda's job offer, if there is one. They both think it will be good for me. But if it weren't for

Beauregard, I doubt I'd even consider it.

I think of Beauregard and how if I start going to Rhonda's aunt's house every day after school, our usual routine will be interrupted. I guess he'll survive, though. Since the weather has been getting cooler, he doesn't go through as much water as he used to. He should be able to wait the extra hour or so for his belly rub as well.

When I step into the beauty salon, Rhonda is busy at the front desk, taking payment from Mrs. Conti, the mother of one of Agnes's friends. Mrs. Conti's hair is in tight ringlets. Must have just had a perm. I catch a whiff of the stinky chemicals too.

Rhonda smiles at me. "I'll be with you in a minute," she says, and continues to chitchat with Mrs. Conti.

So I stare at my fingernails and bite my lip while I wait, my heart beginning a nervous beat. The pounding rhythm at first saying, "I want the job, I want the job, I want the job," then: "No, I don't, no, I don't, no, I don't."

Finally Mrs. Conti wraps up her conversation with Rhonda and turns to leave. "How are you doing, Charlotte?" she asks, suddenly seeing me.

"Fine." I'm afraid she will begin talking and further delay the suspense over my possible job, but she hurries out the door, and I let out a sigh of relief.

"Well, guess what?" Rhonda says, smiling. "You've got yourself a job!"

"I do?"

She nods, putting Mrs. Conti's check in her cash drawer. "To be honest, it was a tough sell. Barth's aunt thinks she can fend for herself after I have the baby, but we finally convinced her it would be for the best." She looks up. "I have a hole in my schedule right now. Want to go on over and meet her? Julie can hold down the fort for a few minutes while I'm gone."

The phone rings, and Rhonda's friend Julie picks it up and waves us on. And without even waiting for my answer, Rhonda ushers me out the door and across the street.

Chapter 24

Rhonda pokes her index finger on the doorbell. "Sometimes it takes a while for her to get to the door to open it," she says. "You've got to be patient, so wait awhile before ringing it again."

A ghostly face stares at me from the side window panel. I let out a startled gasp.

"Oh! Guess this time she must have been right near the door when I rang the bell," Rhonda whispers.

I hear the inside lock being fiddled with, and the door creaks open.

"Come in," says a voice that sounds slightly off-kilter, like an accent from a country I'm not familiar with.

"Go ahead." Rhonda practically pushes me inside. She follows me in, shutting the door behind her.

The three of us stand in the foyer, in front of a worn staircase with a red patterned carpet runner.

"This is Charlotte Hayes," Rhonda says, gesturing at me. "Charlotte, this is Petunia Parker."

I want to make a good impression, so I extend my hand. "Nice to meet you . . ." I pause. Do I call her miss? Mrs.? I quickly decide on Ms. to be safe. "Ms. Parker," I say.

"My right hand doesn't work right," she says briskly.

Oh, dear. Blushing from embarrassment, I withdraw my hand. The stroke, of course. Stupid of me.

"And don't call me Ms.," she says, her voice slightly slurred-sounding.

It's then I realize she doesn't have an accent after all. The left side of her face is drooping, her mouth turned down on the same side. Speech problems from the stroke.

"Oh, I'm sorry," I say.

"Just call me Petunia."

"Like the pig?" I ask.

Oh, great. I can't believe I just said what I said. Daddy likes watching the channel that shows old cartoons a lot, and for some reason I couldn't stop the pig comment from flying out my mouth.

"No, not like the pig. Like the flower. I was named after my father's favorite flower," comes the reply.

Rhonda is smiling at my goof, obviously amused. It looks like she is trying her best not to laugh. But it is hard to tell about Petunia, since her face is half paralyzed. I think I can see the right side of her mouth twitch, though.

Petunia turns her back to us, leans on her cane, and walks away with a strange shuffle hop. "Well, I might as well show you around," she says.

We take a slow tour of the downstairs portion of the house. To the right is a small formal sitting room, which leads into the dining room and then the kitchen. There is a hallway to the left of the kitchen that meanders around the stairway and ends up at the front entry. Petunia's bedroom is at the rear of the house, then a bathroom, and a big living room at the front of the house. So we have, in effect, just made a circle. Everything looks old-fashioned. Like I've stepped into a time warp. But the place is tidy. And so is Petunia. Petunia is kind of pretty, I decide. Her white-gray hair is gathered in a loose twist in the back and she is wearing blush, lipstick, and a purple skirt with a lightweight tan sweater. Noticing these things makes her a little less frightening somehow.

"You have a nice house," I say.

"Thank you," Petunia replies. And I think I catch a certain amount of pride in her voice.

Rhonda explains the routine I am to follow. She gives me the key to Petunia's post office box and tells me that Grater's Groceries down the street has set up an account for Petunia. I'm to get the mail first, then check with Petunia to see if I need to run to the store for anything.

Petunia remains silent through all this. It occurs to me that she is looking just as uncomfortable as I felt a few minutes ago.

"Well, I need to be getting back," Rhonda says, checking her watch. "I have a four o'clock client coming in for a trim." She touches my shoulder. "I'm planning on working until I go into labor, so I won't need you until I have the baby, but I'll call you when I'm headed for the hospital. Okay?"

"Okay," I say, following Rhonda to the door. Petunia and her cane thump after us.

"Good-bye, Aunt Petunia." Rhonda leans over and kisses her on the cheek.

"Good-bye."

I say good-bye, too, but without the kiss, of course, and follow Rhonda out the door.

"Well, that didn't go too bad," Rhonda says, while waiting for the traffic to clear so she can cross the street. "It actually went a lot better than I thought it would. She likes you, I think."

"She does? How do you know?" I definitely couldn't tell.

"Well, it took her years to accept me. Believe me, if she doesn't like you, she lets you know in no uncertain terms."

I don't ask for details.

Beauregard lets out an excited bark when he sees me approach. He knows I'm late. Wish I could explain to him why. There's still a little water left in his bowl, so I don't feel too bad about keeping him waiting. He doesn't even need to take a drink after I fill it full of fresh water. Just flops over for his belly rub.

Once I'm done with the belly rub, I try to ignore the piles of poop that have accumulated since the last time I cleaned up after him, which was only a few days ago, but it's hard to ignore poop 'cause otherwise you'll step in it. I've done that before and don't exactly want a repeat experience, so I go to the garage to get a shovel and stop by the kitchen for a plastic bag. Soon I'm wrinkling my nose as I wedge the shovel between the ground and one of the presents Beauregard left me. Earning that $325 can't come quick enough.

After dinner Daddy visits his breezeway studio, Mama gives Justin Lee his bath, Agnes giggles on the phone with Tom, and I pull up saintrescue.org with a satisfied grin, imagining what it will be like to see Beauregard's profile there.

I click off the Web site, though, when one by one my family starts drifting into the living room: first Mama and Justin Lee with his damp hair, then Agnes, and finally Daddy. Daddy has brought his painting with him. He is holding it gingerly from the back edges where the canvas is stretched and stapled onto the frame. "Needs to dry, but I'm finished," he says. "For you, my sweet." He presents the painting to Mama.

Mama looks happy. Happier than I've seen her in a long time. "Thank you. It's lovely," she says.

And it is kind of lovely. It doesn't exactly look like the picture in the book—much simpler and flatter maybe—but it still looks sort of nice.

While Justin Lee toddles over to his book basket, Mama carefully takes the painting and holds it above the empty space on the wall, right above the couch. "Perfect," she says. She gives Daddy a smooch on the lips. And Daddy, who almost always looks happy, somehow looks even happier than usual.

Justin Lee brings the *B* book over to me. "Char Char," he says. I scoop him onto my lap, breathe in the lingering baby shampoo smell, and start reading to him.

Later Justin Lee is sleeping soundly in his room and Mama and Daddy are watching TV downstairs while I'm waiting for Agnes to come out of the upstairs bathroom so I can have my turn to get ready for bed. After the toilet flushes and I hear water running in the sink, Agnes finally emerges, her cheeks pink from a fresh scrubbing. Before heading in myself, I can't help mentioning to Agnes how Mama is starting to seem more like her old self.

"That painting must have done something," I say. "Or maybe it's because Justin Lee is finally sleeping through the night."

"I think it's mostly because she is getting over her postpartum depression. She was on the phone with Aunt Renee yesterday, and I heard her say she felt like a gray cloud had finally been lifted, that she's feeling much better."

"I was worried about Mama."

"Me, too."

I pause for a moment. "Do you think we should still be worried?"

"Don't think so. Even you noticed she's getting better."

I go to bed knowing I should be feeling pretty good. Mama's coming back to us, I've got a job, and Beauregard will be getting a new home soon.

But I can't help worrying anyway. Rhonda said Petunia Parker likes me.

I'm not so certain that's true.

Chapter 25

Sleepy-eyed, I straggle out to the upstairs hallway and am greeted by a "Morning, birthday girl!" which snaps me out of my just-woke-up fog. It's October 13. I'm the birthday girl.

And there is Mama standing in front of me. She's got on her sweats. And running shoes.

"Daddy's keeping an ear out for Justin Lee while I take a run," she says. "What kind of birthday cake should I make for tonight?"

"Chocolate with fudge icing," I tell her.

"Will do," she says.

I watch her as she jogs down the stairway and disappears from view.

❋ ❋ ❋

At lunch the main topic of conversation is my new job. Luanne and Grace are all excited for me, and I know I should be excited, too. But I can't help wondering if Petunia Parker will make things unpleasant for me.

"Petunia's a weird name," Luanne says. "But kind of cute." She takes a bite out of her pizza slice.

"I know. I asked her if she was named after a pig."

Grace's mouth drops open. "You didn't."

"I did." I nod, still blushing from the memory.

"Was she mad?" Luanne places her slice of pizza back down on the pink plastic school tray.

"I couldn't tell. Her face kind of droops. And she doesn't get around too good either. That's why Rhonda thinks she needs my help." I take a bite of my own pizza. "Problem is, I'm not sure she actually wants my help."

I blow out the twelve candles on my chocolate fudge cake and watch as the tiny trails of smoke disappear.

There are no birthday presents nearby waiting to be opened, but before I can cut the cake, Daddy shoves a card at me. It's a funny one with a monkey on it. Daddy picked it out, I assume, and it's stuffed with two twenties.

"Thanks," I say.

"You can always change your mind, you know," Daddy tells me. "You could buy something for yourself with the money if you want."

"No. I'm buying Killer," I reply.

Agnes looks at me like I'm crazy for saying so, but instead of making a smart comment, she asks me to hurry up and cut the cake.

Soon we all have nice-size chunks on our plates. Even Justin Lee has a small piece on his tray. He pokes a finger in the icing and licks his finger.

"You're next in line," Mama tells him.

He squashes his piece of cake with an open hand and plasters half of it to his mouth. Justin Lee's birthday is in early December; he'll be a big one-year-old then.

The phone rings.

"I'll get it." Agnes jumps up. A few seconds later she says, "Charlotte, it's for you."

It's Rhonda's husband. "The baby's coming early," he says, his voice all quick and excited. "Rhonda wants to know if you can start tomorrow."

"Sure," I say.

"Aunt Petunia will expect you around three-thirty then. Visit a bit, and you can leave at four-thirty."

"Okay. Good luck with the baby," I say.

"And good luck with Aunt Petunia." Rhonda's husband gives a nervous laugh.

I hang up the phone not quite sure if the nervous laugh is over his wife's impending birth or me having to put up with an old lady named after a flower.

Chapter 26

The walk to Petunia's after school is a windy one. Stray orange and yellow leaves scoot across the sidewalk, and the sky is a deep blue. I stop by the post office and fish through my backpack for Petunia's key, which I placed inside a small zippered compartment. I find the key among loose change and sticks of gum, locate Petunia's PO box—number 82—among rows and rows of similar boxes, then stick the key in with a twist. I collect a few business-size envelopes, and I'm on my way again.

I cut over to Fenton Street, and before I know it I'm on the porch of the weathered yellow house with crooked green shutters. It takes Petunia a while to answer the front door. I remembered Rhonda's advice not to be impatient, so I don't ring the doorbell twice, but when the door finally opens, Petunia still looks upset over something.

"Come in," she says, her voice not exactly welcoming.

I step inside and hand her the small bundle of mail I collected from her PO box.

"Thank you," she says stiffly, placing the envelopes on a small foyer table near the stairway.

"So what did Rhonda have?" I ask.

"A girl. Amber Rose."

"That's pretty. And she's named after a flower, like you."

"Well, that's better than being named after a farm-yard animal, I suppose."

Petunia's back is turned, and she's looking through the envelopes she placed on the foyer table, so I can't tell if she is trying to make a joke about my foot-in-mouth episode two days ago or if she is trying to make me feel bad.

Do I laugh or do I not laugh? Do I make a silly

comeback or ignore the comment? I end up remaining silent.

Petunia turns around to face me. "You may go sit in the parlor."

Parlor. Would that be the big living room to the left? Or the small sitting area to the right that has two wingback chairs and a couch?

I stand there with a confused look on my face. Petunia leans on her cane and thumps toward one of the wingback chairs. I follow her.

She sits in one of the blue velvet chairs, which is placed in front of a big picture window, so I settle onto the couch across the way. That way I'm not too close and yet not too far away.

"Do you need anything from Grater's?" I ask.

"No. I'm fine. I'll need milk tomorrow. Maybe a can of soup."

I'm sort of disappointed I don't have to make a grocery run. I already feel like I need a break from Petunia. An ornate cuckoo clock hangs on the wall nearby, ticking away. I've been here only five minutes. Fifty-five more to go. What am I going to do to fill the time?

I clear my throat. "So Rhonda and the baby are doing fine?"

"From what I've heard."

A long pause.

"I think I'll read," Petunia finally says. There is a thick book next to a lamp on a small round table by her chair. She picks the book up, finds her place, and starts reading without a further word.

From the front cover I can tell it's a murder mystery. A glinting knife and a crumpled silhouette of a body. This does nothing to ease my discomfort.

I unzip my backpack, which I placed at my feet, and find my own library book. I'm still reading the one about a girl named Maddie lost in the woods. She was on the verge of being found when I left off, and I have only a few chapters to go until the end.

Twenty-five minutes later I am finished. Maddie has survived her adventure in the woods and as a result no longer seems like a spoiled rich girl.

I just don't know if I can survive my remaining thirty minutes with Petunia.

Petunia appears to be engrossed with her book. The

afternoon sun is shining from behind her, and again, like the first time we met, I am struck by how pretty she is. Tiny nose. Tiny chin. Big eyes. She's wearing a rose-colored skirt today, and a blue knit sweater, and she has a small bit of makeup on. I find myself wondering what she looked like when she was younger.

I glance around the room, trying to see if there are any pictures displayed. I don't find one of Petunia, but on the side table by the couch is a framed picture of the house. It looks different. Cheerful. Probably because the house was freshly painted. I know that because a man is standing in the front yard, and he's grinning and holding up a paint can. It's an old color photo, and the yellow of the house reminds me of a baby chicken. Not garish or bright, but a warm and fuzzy shade.

I want to pick up the picture to get a closer look, but I don't dare.

A voice makes me jump. "Can I get you anything to drink? A snack?" Petunia is staring at me, the murder mystery closed on her lap. "Lemonade and a cookie?"

I am thirsty and hungry, so I say, "Yes, please."

"Come with me to the kitchen then."

Seated at the kitchen table, I feel a little guilty for saying yes to Petunia's offer. Considering her stroke, it's no small task for Petunia to get me a cookie and pour me a glass of lemonade. Shouldn't I be taking care of her and not the other way around? But for some reason, Petunia doesn't seem as gruff as she did earlier.

Still, right at the moment I take the first bite out of my iced molasses cookie, Petunia tells me she needs to write out some bills. She makes her way over to a desk with cubbyholes in the corner of the kitchen, and the only sound I hear is my self-conscious crunching.

By the time I leave, a ten-dollar bill tucked in my pocket, I believe Petunia and I have exchanged all of ten words.

Chapter 27

After a week I believe Petunia's and my daily word count is even less. It's not a hard job, but it's certainly an uncomfortable one. It's not that Petunia is mean exactly. It's more like she just doesn't want me there. So when she has me go to Grater's to pick up something like a loaf of bread or a half gallon jug of skim milk for her, I walk verrrrry sloooowly. I also take the time to read all the headlines of the magazine covers by the checkout, even though I'm not really interested in what celebrities are up to. I do anything to take up time; otherwise each second back at Petunia's drags by forever.

The early-morning bell rings for school and Grace

rushes into the room. She flashes a smile as she passes my desk. I notice something different . . .

"You got your braces!" I say.

"Yep." She nods, stopping in her tracks. "Mom says you and Luanne can come for a sleepover tomorrow night since it's Friday. We can rent movies or something."

"Okay. Sounds fun."

"Hey, Grace. Braces with pink bands. Cool," says Becca, who sits at the desk across from mine.

"The orthodontist says next time I can change the color," Grace replies.

"That's neat."

A few more kids come up to study Grace's braces. She has become a regular member of our class now, no longer someone to be stared or whispered at. Roxanne, Madison, and Becca have actually started joining our lunch table. It's a bit crowded, but no one seems to mind.

Petunia does not need any groceries today. She sits in the blue velvet wingback chair, reading another murder mystery. This one has a gun on the front.

I have finished another two library books since I started my job here but haven't made it back to the library to return them and get more reading material. So I am stuck with nothing to do. Not even any homework. I decide to get out a school notebook and do some doodling on the back pages I hope I won't need. I stare at the framed photo of Petunia's house and begin sketching it out. Once I get the house looking good, I start in on the grinning man with the paint can, but I feel like I need a closer look to get the details right.

Since Petunia seems so in tune with her book, I pick up the framed photo of her house that sits on the nearby side table.

"That's my father."

Startled, I nearly drop the photo.

Petunia has her book folded on her lap.

"Oh." I quickly close my notebook with my free hand, not wanting Petunia to see what I have drawn.

"He painted the house himself. Took him a

month. He was so proud of how it looked when he was finished."

"I can tell," I say. I place the picture back on the table. "It does look nice."

"He died the very next day. Heart attack."

Oh, dear. What can I say to that? Finally I get out the words "I'm sorry."

"I know the house looks bad from the outside now." Petunia sighs, shrugs, and reopens her book.

After the brief bit of talking we did, the silence in the room somehow seems strangely bothersome.

"Well, why haven't you repainted the house?" I ask, before realizing how rude I must sound. I want to clamp my hand over my mouth, but it is way too late.

Petunia looks up from her book. "I guess, in a way, it would seem like repainting over the memory of my father. I did go to the paint store once. Collected dozens and dozens of paint chips. Blue ones, tan ones, red ones, even pink ones. But I was so overwhelmed by all the color choices it just ended up being easier to make no decision at all."

The fact that Petunia is actually talking to me, almost confiding in me, makes me suddenly brave. I gesture at the picture of her father and the freshly painted house. "Do you have other pictures I could see?" I ask.

"There's an album in the living room. Bookshelves by the fireplace. You may go and get it if you wish."

I slip my notebook into my backpack and make my way to the living room.

By the time I return with the photo album, Petunia is busy reading again. I sit at my usual place on the couch, wondering if she'll join me to explain some of the pictures, but she remains seated in her wingback chair.

Chapter 28

It's hard not to pester Petunia with a million questions as I make my way through the photo album, but I don't want to pry or appear nosy. So I quietly leaf through the pages, being grateful that at least I have something to do to pass the time.

It looks like Petunia had a brother a few years older than her, but I gather something happened to her mother. She's in a few baby pictures, but then she disappears, poof, just like that. Did she die? Run off with a boyfriend? There are lots of happy pictures, though, of Petunia, her father, and her brother. And she was beautiful. There are pictures of her in her teen years looking glamorous, dressed up like she was going to a dance, with a handsome boy at her side. Pictures of her as a young woman, looking serious in a businesslike narrow skirt and jacket and then grinning in a bathing suit at the beach with others her age. But there are no wedding pictures to be found. The last picture in the album is another shot of the freshly painted house and her father. I close the album.

"Are you ready for some lemonade and a snack?" Petunia asks. "Oatmeal raisin cookies today. Fresh from the box."

"That sounds good. Thanks for letting me look at the photo album."

"Sure." Petunia begins her unsteady gait to the kitchen.

Once I get settled at the table with my cookie and glass of lemonade, I expect Petunia to busy herself with something like she always does, but instead she sits herself down across from me.

"I don't think it's fair for you to have to come here every day after school," she says. "I'm sure you would rather be spending time with your friends than being bored to death here. I know Rhonda said you needed to earn some money. But all I really need is for someone to get the mail or run to Grater's for me. You really don't need to stay here until four-thirty. You can start leaving early if you want; I'll still pay you the same. Rhonda worries about my being lonely, but I'm fine, really."

Now a few days ago I would have jumped at such an offer. But for some reason, after looking through the photo album and talking with her a bit, I want to find out more about Petunia Parker. "I don't mind being here," I say. I take a sip of lemonade.

"Are you sure?" she asks.

I nod.

"Well, how about a game of gin rummy then?" Petunia says. "You have a half hour left, and my latest murder mystery has been solved."

Petunia gets a deck of cards from her kitchen desk drawer. She hands them to me. "I can't shuffle any-more, so you do the honors."

I start shuffling the cards.

"What I really love playing is euchre, but you need four people for that," Petunia says. "Goodness, it's been a good fifteen years or so since I've played that game."

It's difficult for Petunia to play. Basically she has the use of only one hand, her left, but she manages by setting the cards facedown after she looks at them, withdrawing the one she wants to play, and picking the rest up again by sliding them toward the table edge.

By four-thirty I end up winning one game of rummy. Petunia wins four. And I've got an idea brewing for tomorrow. A surprise for Petunia Parker.

Chapter 29

The walk home from Petunia's is a cold one. The wind is downright nasty, and I stuff my hands in my coat pockets, wishing I were wearing gloves. By the time I reach our driveway, I notice a few stray snow-flakes falling from the sky. October 21, our first snow of the season. A little early to have anything more than a brief flurry, so I doubt it will amount to much. I'd really like to go right inside and get warmed up, but Beauregard needs tending to.

Beauregard's tail starts wagging to beat the band the moment he sees me. After filling up his water bowl, instead of giving him a belly rub, I wrap my arms around his neck, hugging him just to get warm. His fur feels nice and toasty against my cheek. He doesn't seem to mind. But when I start to walk away, he quickly collapses on the ground, belly up.

"All right," I say, walking back. "A hug *and* a belly rub. I guess today's your lucky day."

When I go through the breezeway, I notice the same blank canvas sitting on the windowsill that has been taking up space for a while. Daddy never did start a new painting after the flowers in the vase one. I pick up the how-to-paint book Daddy left on top of a cluttered pile of stuff, take it up to my room, and read it until I hear Mama's voice calling me to come set the table for dinner.

A bit later, as I'm dipping a slice of bread into a puddle of gravy, I mention to Daddy how cold it is. "Don't you think maybe we should bring Killer inside? At least at night?" I ask.

"No dog in the house," Mama says sternly.

"But . . . " I begin.

Daddy waves his hand at me, shooing away

my attempt to fight the issue. "Are you kidding? Charlotte, didn't I tell you those dogs were bred to rescue people up on the snow-covered mountains of Switzerland? He'll be fine."

I wasn't happy with Daddy's answer, but I knew arguing wasn't going to change his mind. He's stubborn that way. Mama, too. I decide to ask about something else I've been wondering about. "You going to paint anymore, Daddy?"

"Naw. Don't think so."

"But you did such a nice job with your first painting," Mama says, surprised.

"Oh, I enjoyed it, I guess, but it's such a hassle getting everything set up. And you can do only one layer at a time. And don't get me started on cleaning those brushes afterward; I just don't have the patience for it. It's a shame 'cause I really do have the talent for it." Daddy grins. "I'm a regular Vincent van Gogh, but the world will have to settle for just one of my paintings."

"Could I use your paint set sometime then, Daddy?" I ask.

Daddy nods.

❁ ❁ ❁

The house is dark, the clock glows 12:20 A.M., but I can't sleep. The wind is howling outside, and I'm thinking about Beauregard and his too small doghouse. Fall here in Greater Oaks started out like summer; now it isn't close to being over, and you'd think it was winter already. I get up and look out my window. Daddy always leaves the back porch light on before going to bed, and I can see scattered snowflakes whipping around the light. Still, it's too dark to see Beauregard clearly from up here, and I wonder if he's shivering. I bet those rescue dogs in Switzerland had decent shelter, when they weren't doing their jobs, and got a break from the cold. I wish I could bring Beauregard up to my room, but someone would be sure to hear him clumping up the stairs with those big clumsy paws of his.

I slip on a pair of fuzzy slippers and grab my pillow from the bed and my alarm clock, too. I creep out of my room and tiptoe down the stairs, careful to step over the creaking fourth stair from the bottom. I place my pillow on one end of the couch, set my alarm clock for 5:00 A.M., and then stuff it under my pillow so the sound will be muffled when it goes off. I feel my way through the kitchen, careful not to bump into anything, and quietly unlatch the lock on the breezeway door. Once outside, I race over to Beauregard, the wind stinging my cheeks and making my eyes water. There's no snow gathered on the ground, but everything feels hard and frozen under my feet. I can only imagine what it feels like for Beauregard, lying out in the open, exposed. I unclip his chain, grab his collar, and lead him back to the breezeway door.

"You be good," I say, before letting him in. I keep a firm grip on his collar and guide him to the couch. Pushing on his lower back, I make him sit; then I softly pat the floor to get him to lie down. I settle onto the couch.

"Good night, Beauregard," I whisper, putting my face close to his.

He licks my cheek.

Oh, gross.

I fall asleep, my hand clutched around his nylon collar, soft fur wedged between my fingers.

Chapter 30

When the alarm goes off, it takes a moment for me to realize I am not in my room. As soon as I remember why I'm on the couch, I panic, but then I feel Beauregard's fur wound around my fingers. He obviously didn't go roaming around the house in the middle of the night. I peer over the side of the couch at Beauregard. He has his head on his front paws, and he is in such a deep sleep I can barely notice him breathing.

"Come on, sleeping beauty," I whisper, nudging him awake. He clambers to his feet, and I steer him through the living room to the kitchen. His nails click across the linoleum floor, but I'm hoping everyone upstairs is still sleeping soundly and won't notice. Once outside, I find the wind has died down, and it no longer feels so bitterly cold. I chain Beauregard up again, go back inside, gather my pillow and alarm clock from the couch, check for any drool that needs wiping up, and steal back up to my room.

Later that day, when I show up on Petunia's porch, I'm not by myself. I've got Luanne and Grace with me. They've walked here with me after school, and then at four-thirty they'll walk back home with me so I can take care of Beauregard. After that, Mrs. Walters will pick us up, and we'll have our Friday night sleepover at Grace's house.

Last night, after dinner, when I called Grace to make all the arrangements, Mrs. Walters had to get on the phone and ask a bunch of questions. When I explained that Petunia was an eighty-three-year-old who had had a stroke, Mrs. Walters finally figured Grace would be safe. Of course I didn't mention any- thing about the murder mysteries Petunia loves to read. Still, once Mrs. Walters was done talking to me, she asked to speak to Mama just to make sure every-thing would be all right.

While we wait for Petunia to answer the door, Luanne sticks her finger out to give the bell a second ring. I push her hand away. "It takes her a while," I say. "She'll open the door. Just wait."

A few seconds later the door does open. And Petunia is so surprised to see Grace and Luanne she just stares at them, speechless.

"These are my friends," I say. "We're here to learn how to play euchre."

Chapter 31

Euchre, we find out, is played in pairs. Me and Petunia partner up against Grace and Luanne. It takes a while to get the hang of it, but once I figure it out, it's really fun.

So we snack on oatmeal raisin cookies, drink lemonade, and play euchre.

And we talk. Even Petunia talks. She started to open up a tiny bit yesterday, but there's something about playing cards that loosens her up.

Luanne ends up asking Petunia what kind of job she had.

Petunia stares at her hand of cards, trying to decide

186

which one to play. "Well, my father was the founder and president of the Greater Oaks Community Bank. I wanted to follow in his footsteps, so I went to business school, got my master's degree, and went to work in the bank here when I graduated. Worked there fifteen years and knew how to run things inside and out. When my father died, I assumed I would take over the reins of the business. But the board of directors thought differently. They didn't want a woman president." Petunia lays down her cards, withdraws the one she has chosen, and places it at the center of the table. Then she scoops the rest of her hand up again.

"That's terrible," says Grace.

"Well, things were different back then, but I didn't let it hold me back. I up and quit the bank my father founded and went to work as a vice-president for a bank in New York City. Eventually they made me president. So everything worked out well for me after all. I had a wonderful career, and then I retired and came back here to live; I had never sold the house."

"New York," Grace says. She throws down her

card and wins the trick, so she gathers up the pile of played cards. "Oh, I love New York. My family has visited several times. So much to do."

"Oh, I had a grand time. Broadway shows, the opera, ballet, museums. And I had quite a few beaux, you know."

"Beaux?" Luanne asks. She looks up from her cards.

"Boyfriends," Petunia says. "Was even proposed to several times. But I declined."

"Why?" I ask.

"I guess what it boiled down to was I liked living by myself," she replies. "I was set in my ways. Still am." She gives a lopsided grin.

As the game goes on, we learn that Petunia's mother ran off to become an actress when she was only two. Her mother landed a few roles but never became famous and never returned home.

"I think that is why I was so close to my father," she says.

Before long I end up telling her the whole story of Beauregard and how I am going to use the money I'm earning to help buy him from my father. "After I'm done working for you, I'll only need to earn twenty-five dollars more. Then I'm going to give him to a rescue group," I say.

"When I lived in New York, one of my boyfriends had a Saint Bernard named Clyde. Can you imagine a Saint Bernard in an apartment? But it worked. They lived near Central Park and went out for long daily romps. Oh, how I adored Clyde. In fact I almost married that young man for his dog!" Petunia ends up taking the next trick and gathers up the small pile of cards. "You know I'd buy your Beauregard in a minute, but I'm in no shape to take care of a dog, I'm afraid. Anyway, I'm glad I'm able to help in some way. If you have trouble coming up with the remaining twenty-five dollars after your job is done here, let me know. I'm sure I can find something for you to do around here to help earn the rest of the money."

"Thanks," I tell her. "That would be great."

Between the talking and Petunia reminding us about euchre rules, we get only one game in by four-thirty. Grace and Luanne are declared the winners, since they reached ten points first.

And it is decided that Fridays will be euchre day from now on. Even when Rhonda gets back to work and doesn't need me anymore, we will meet at Petunia's to play euchre every Friday afternoon.

We have just finished watching a movie about a figure skater at Grace's house and are on our way up to her room. We have stomachs full of popcorn and are in our pj's already even though it's still early in the evening. It is a sleepover after all. Figaro decided to keep me company during the movie; he lay right by my side, and it wasn't until the credits were rolling that I realized I had absently stroked him through most of the movie.

"You sure you're not a dog person?" Grace asks.

"Hey, I can't help it if your dog likes me best," I say as we tramp up the stairs. "What should we do next?" I ask.

"You can braid our hair," Luanne says.

And so, as I'm sitting on Grace's big canopy bed, weaving Luanne's hair, we talk about our day with Petunia.

"She's nice," Luanne says. "I don't see why you thought it was difficult spending time with her at first."

"Well, she doesn't warm up easy. But then neither did Grace when we first met her," I say, grinning.

Grace laughs. "I was so scared when I started school here. I kind of froze up like a window mannequin."

"Do you think Petunia was kind of scared when you started going over to her house?" Luanne asks. "Do you think that's why she didn't talk much?"

I stop braiding for a few seconds. "In a way. She's very independent. I mean, just think, she was a bank president. And now she has to depend on a twelve-year-old to get her mail and groceries. I think she's used to taking care of things, not being taken care of."

"Maybe that's why she was able to enjoy herself today," Grace says. "'Cause she was teaching *us* something."

"I think you're right."

Outside Grace's bedroom window shines an almost full moon in a clear sky. No rain or snow. Not too cold either. Beauregard should be okay in his too small doghouse tonight, so I should be able to relax and enjoy myself, too. Heck, I don't even have to worry about the twenty-five dollars I thought I'd need to make after Rhonda gets back to checking in on Petunia, since Petunia said she'd come up with something else for me to do to earn it.

I think in the helping-out department Petunia has me beat.

Chapter 32

In the middle of November I ring Petunia's door-bell, thinking what a difference a month can make. A month ago I started my job with Petunia and we barely spoke to each other. Now I'm her friend—and Grace and Luanne, too! A month ago Beauregard slept outside. Now he sleeps snug and warm and cozy on the living room floor. I usually stay up reading until midnight, using a flashlight under the covers so my parents won't know, then sneak him in. It's a pain because I have to get up early every morning, too, to put him back outside before anyone gets up, but I know it's a temporary situation. Soon he'll have a new home. I've already earned $200 of the $325 I need!

Also, a month ago Mama still wasn't quite herself, but now she's doing great; she even manages to run at least a couple of mornings a week. A month ago Agnes was dating Tom, but now she has a new boyfriend named Hunter. A month ago Justin Lee used his hands to eat. Now he can use a spoon. Well, sort of. And Daddy went from artist to nonartist. And me? Well, I've picked up the painting thing where Daddy left off. In fact I just finished my first painting last night. It's a picture of our dogwood tree out back and the blue doghouse. I took my time, unlike Daddy, and really studied the how-to book before starting.

I sketched out each stage of the picture. I experimented with mixing colors until I got the perfect shades I wanted. I used layers, starting with the background and slowly adding details. In the end it turned out terrific. Everyone says so. Daddy did ask me why Beauregard isn't in the picture. I just shrugged and said he'd be too hard to paint. But I actually painted what I hope will be a scene from the future. Only two more weeks to go, and I'll have most of the money it will take to buy Beauregard.

I shuffle in the cold and wait a few more minutes, resisting the urge to ring the doorbell again. Petunia seems to be taking longer than usual. I pull my cap down, so it covers the bottom of my ears. My breath comes out in steamy puffs. Hope she comes to the door soon. I peer into the side window panel.

And there is Petunia sprawled out on the floor at the foot of the stairs, looking like one of the murdered bodies on the covers of the books she reads.

I open my mouth to scream, but no noise comes out.

Chapter 33

I run as fast as my feet can carry me over to Rhonda's
Cut and Curl. I throw open the door with such force
that I startle Julie, and she nearly clips a huge hunk out
of some poor man's hair.

"Sorry," she says to him. She frowns at me.

I gasp for air. "It's Rhonda's aunt. Petunia. I think—I
think she's dead."

Julie drops the scissors, races to the phone, and dials
911.

And then I start bawling.

Knowing an ambulance is on the way, I sprint back
over to Petunia's, tears streaming down my face. I peek

in and pound furiously at the door, screaming her name over and over again. That's when I see her raise her head up ever so slightly. But all I can see is a twist of white-gray hair, since her face is pointed toward the stairs.

"Help is on the way," I shout, hoping she can hear my voice through the door. I think I see her nod.

I just stand there, helpless, straining my ears for the sound of a siren.

When the ambulance finally comes, I stand on the front porch, making sure not to get in the way but also trying to see what is going on through the busted-open front door.

Petunia is moaning, unable to talk. Suddenly Barth, Rhonda's husband, is at my side.

"Julie called. Got here as soon as I could, drove like a madman. Is she okay?" he asks.

"Don't know."

Barth yells to the man and woman hovering over Petunia. "Gus, Shelly, it's Barth. What happened?"

"Broken hip as far as we can tell. Looks like your aunt took a spill down the last few steps, maybe," the woman says, glancing toward him.

Minutes later Petunia is carried out on a gurney and loaded into the back of the ambulance. Barth is allowed to climb into the front, next to the driver, to make the trip with her.

I watch the ambulance until it disappears down the street, wondering if I will ever get to see Petunia again.

As soon as I get home, I call Grace and Luanne to let them know what has happened to Petunia. Both come over to my house to wait for news of how she is doing. Finally Rhonda calls around five-thirty to thank me for getting help and to give an update on Petunia's condition. She tells me Petunia is in a hospital in West Townfield and will be there for a while; after that she will go into a rehabilitation center. She did break her hip but seems fine otherwise. Still, with her age, dangerous complications can set in, Rhonda says, and even if they don't, it will take months for her to recover well enough to be able to live at home again.

Grace and Luanne are just as relieved as I am that

Petunia will be okay. Mama orders pizza, and they both stay for dinner before going home.

I end up being so preoccupied about Petunia and what happened that it doesn't hit me until I'm on my way out to sneak Beauregard in for the night: I don't have a job anymore. That means I will be $125 short of buying Beauregard. Every time I think something is going to work, it takes a turn for the worse.

Maybe Beauregard and me are cursed.

I lie on the couch in the still, dark house, dangling my arm off the side and stroking the back of Beauregard's neck. "I'm sorry," I whisper.

Beauregard lifts his head and places his chin on the couch cushion. He stares at me as if to say, "I know. It's okay."

Then he sighs and closes his eyes.

All of a sudden I hear a creak on the stairs. I bolt upright. There is enough light coming in through the windows that I can see Agnes at the foot of the stairs.

"What are you doing down here?" she asks in a voice loud enough I'm worried Mama or Daddy may hear.

"Shhh!" I wave her over to where I am so I can whisper to her instead of talking normally.

Once she reaches the couch, she sees Beauregard. "You are going to be in such trouble," she says in a hushed voice. "You know Mama and Daddy don't want that dog in the house." She sits down beside me.

"It's cold outside. I felt sorry for him. You won't tell, will you?"

Beauregard lays his head on her lap. She scratches behind his ear. "No, I won't tell," she says.

"What are you doing up?" I ask.

"Couldn't sleep. Thought a glass of milk would help." She gets up and rubs at her nightgown. "Eww, he drooled on me." She turns toward the kitchen, then turns back to me. "I'm glad you're buying Killer from Daddy so we can keep him. I know I don't spend much time with him, but I do like him. He's a nice dog," she says, "even if he does drool."

"I don't think I'm going to be able to buy Killer," I tell her. "With Petunia in the hospital, I won't be able to pay Daddy by the deadline. He's gonna sell Killer, I just know it." I pause. "Can you keep another secret?" I ask.

"Sure."

"I really wasn't buying Killer so we could keep him. I was going to give him to a rescue group."

"You were?"

I nod. "He deserves a better life. And I'm tired of having to take care of him."

Agnes bends down to pat Beauregard's head. "I always thought you enjoyed being around Killer."

I shrug. "Not really." I pat Beauregard on the head, too. "Still, I'm worried. What if Killer ends up in an even worse home if Daddy sells him?"

"Maybe Daddy won't have to sell him. Maybe you can find another job. Or maybe you can ask Daddy for an extension on the deadline; you've already earned most of the money, haven't you?"

I doubt if I could find another job in the amount of time I have left. It was difficult enough finding the one with Petunia. But maybe Daddy would give me an extension on my deadline. "Thanks, Agnes," I say, and I feel better after talking to her.

Chapter 34

While waiting for the school day to start, Grace, Luanne, and I discuss Petunia.

"We should send her a get well card," Luanne says.

"And flowers," Grace adds. "I've had a lot of fun the past few Fridays; I'm going to miss playing euchre at her house."

The bell sounds, and Mrs. Delenor claps her hands and tells us all to take our seats.

I wish there were something I could do for Petunia besides sending her a card or giving her flowers. I knew she'd be miserable in the hospital, having all those strangers taking care of her. She loved her house. She loved being independent. And both those things were taken away from her.

By the end of the school day I have decided on something special I can do for Petunia. I call Rhonda as soon as I get home. I ask about Petunia. And about Amber Rose, too. Both are doing fine. Then I ask for a favor. I can't give Petunia her independence back, but I thought of a way, with Rhonda's help, I could bring a bit of home to her.

I stand back and squint, full of pride.

It's the middle of December, and I have been working on my new masterpiece for four weeks straight, getting the colors just exactly right: fluffy chick yellow and a green deeper than grass but lighter than pine tree needles. I studied the framed picture of Petunia's house that Rhonda brought over, and then I studied what I did on the canvas. Early on I wondered if I should attempt drawing and painting in Petunia's father at the side of the house. I worried if I couldn't do a good job with her father, it would ruin the painting. I decided to go ahead and try and ended up pleased with the results. The scale is perfect. The shading is perfect. Right down to the proud smile on Mr. Parker's face, it's perfect. I replicated the photo. But it's bigger . . . and in a way, even though the colors are exact, it's more brilliant, lively. All that's left for me to do is let it dry up a bit more and then send it to the rehabilitation center with Rhonda or Barth. They take turns making the hour trip to visit Petunia every day. One stays home with Amber Rose while the other drives to West Townfield. I'll just send the painting up with whoever's going.

At first Mama actually talked about taking me, Luanne, and Grace up for a visit, but when Rhonda mentioned it to Petunia, she said she'd rather not have us see her in her current condition. Mama said we should honor her wishes. I remember how tidy Petunia always looked: hair never messy, coordinated sweaters and skirts, the perfect amount of makeup on. Maybe Mama is right, though I think I'd still like to see her anyway.

I begin cleaning my brushes with turpentine. Daddy spoke the truth; cleaning up is a pain when it comes to paint with oils. But creating something that has meaning is worth the work.

Chapter 35

On Christmas morning I'm not exactly full of Christmas cheer. I know there's no way I can get the $125 I need by January 9, my deadline for buying Beauregard.

A few days earlier I asked Mama and Daddy for money instead of a gift for my Christmas present. But Mama said she had already bought my gifts, and she wasn't about to return them. I also asked Daddy for an extension on the payment due date, like Agnes suggested.

"Maybe when Petunia moves back to the house, Rhonda will need me to help," I said.

But Daddy said, "Sorry. A deal is a deal. If we don't follow through, it won't teach you anything now, will it?"

So I've resigned myself to the fact Daddy will be selling Beauregard. I asked him to at least try to make sure he has a good home this time. "You could put 'home inspection required' in the ad," I said. And I told him some questions he should ask when people called.

"Home inspection?" Daddy laughed. "I don't think so. And I'm not going to insult the buyer and ask a bunch of nosy questions. Anyway, I'm sure he'll end up being taken care of just as well as he is here. I wouldn't worry."

Somehow I didn't find his words very encouraging.

Right now I'm sitting on the floor, in front of the tree, right between Justin Lee and Agnes.

Justin Lee seems to be getting the idea that when you unwrap something, a toy appears. Actually he's getting the idea a little too well, because when he finally runs out of presents to open, he begins to cry.

Daddy grins, swooping him up and tickling him. "What? You think you're the only little boy on Santa's list?"

Agnes is happily surrounded by opened boxes of clothes.

Mama has been clicking away, taking pictures, and she stops for a moment. "Why haven't you opened your gifts yet, Charlotte?" she asks.

"Just enjoying watching everyone else." I force a grin and grab the biggest box in my pile and start to tear into the green paper decorated with red stars. I sent my gift to Petunia, the painting, with Rhonda a few days ago, and I find myself wondering what her reaction was. I'm more curious about that than I am about the contents of the box I'm opening.

The doorbell rings, and everyone looks up surprised. Who could it be on Christmas morning?

Mama goes over to open the door, and there's Rhonda.

I put my half-opened box down, and thoughts about Petunia getting my painting slip away. Instead I'm wondering if Rhonda has bad news about Petunia. Maybe she had another stroke. Or a heart attack. Rhonda did say there could be complications because of her age. My heart starts pounding.

"Come on in," Mama says.

"Oh, I can't stay. Barth and Amber Rose are waiting for me in the car; we're on the way to my sister's to exchange presents. Anyway, we were celebrating Christmas Eve with Petunia last night, and she gave me this to give to Charlotte." Rhonda holds out a box loosely tied with a silver ribbon.

I jump up and get the box. I slip off the silver ribbon, open the box, and find a check, made out to me. The check is for $125. There's also a note written on red stationery paper. The handwriting is pretty messy, but I'm able to make out the words.

> I can't accept the painting as a gift. It is a wonderful piece of art, and you should be compensated.
>
> Petunia

"Petunia absolutely loves the painting," Rhonda says. "It makes her room look much more cheerful.

It has even made Petunia herself more cheerful. She has it propped up on the dresser across from her bed, where she can always see it. It's really motivating her to work hard to get home."

"I can't take this," I say. I try to give the check back to Rhonda, but she refuses to take it.

"If you think I'm about to give this back to her, you've got another thing coming." Rhonda laughs. "I'm not going to upset her like that." With that Rhonda waves good-bye to everyone and bustles out the door.

"Why don't you go ahead and open your gifts now?" Mama tells me.

I stuff the check into my bathrobe pocket, go back, sit on the floor, and tear off the remaining wrapping paper from the big box. Seconds later I'm staring at what it contains. Several blank canvases and a sketch pad. I almost start crying. Perfect. I clutch the sketch pad to my chest. "Thanks, Mama. Daddy."

"Don't thank us." Daddy grins. "Thank Santa."

Though I'm itching to use either my new sketch pad or canvas, I end up spending most of the rest of the day looking at that check Rhonda dropped off.

The painting was a gift. Somehow I don't feel right accepting money for it. For a while I consider finding the address for the rehabilitation center and sending it back. But then I find myself remembering how Petunia always seemed most at ease when she was being useful. Like when she was getting me cookies and lemonade. Or when she was teaching me, Luanne, and Grace euchre. Or when she learned the money she was paying me was really helping *me* out. There's no doubt in my mind what she intended that check to be used for. It was for the exact amount I needed.

I figure there is no way Petunia could be feeling useful in the rehabilitation center. I'm sure everyone there is concentrating on making her better, helping *her* out. But I could make her feel needed and necessary because in this very instance she is. Both to me and to Beauregard.

I run upstairs to my room and gather up all the

cash I have saved so far. I quickly scribble my name on the back of the check from Petunia and run back downstairs. I hand the cash and the check over to Daddy.

"I'm paid in full," I tell Daddy. "Killer is mine."

Chapter 36

I wait until a few days after Christmas to tell Mama and Daddy my plans for Beauregard.

"A rescue group? Killer doesn't need rescued! No one beats him or even raises their voice to him. He's not abused," Daddy says.

"I know. But he doesn't get much attention. And he loves people, Daddy. He could go to a family that really wants him. A family that won't keep him chained up."

"I still don't think we need to be giving him to a rescue group," Daddy says.

Mama crosses her arms and gives Daddy a firm look. "Didn't you tell Charlotte that a deal is a deal when she wanted an extension?"

"Yes, but—"

Mama cuts him off. "Well, Charlotte paid for Killer fair and square. He belongs to her now, and she can do as she pleases with him."

"Yes, and if you go back on your deal, you wouldn't be teaching me anything now, would you, Daddy?" I say, remembering the lecture he gave me.

Daddy starts to laugh. And I know I won the argument.

Even though I was out earlier to feed and water him, I throw on a hat, coat, and boots to go out back to see Beauregard.

"It's a done deal," I tell him. "You will be on your way soon to a new family, a new home." I start clapping my hands and jumping like a maniac, and soon I've got him all excited. He's jumping around and running back and forth.

We're doing a victory dance, Beauregard and I.

The dog days of Charlotte Hayes are drawing to a close.

Two days before the New Year, Mama and I take Beauregard to the animal shelter. Kathleen is surprised to see him. "Did he get loose again?" she asks, remembering how I brought in the same dog back in the fall.

I explain the whole thing to her: how we aren't able to give him a good home and how I've been wanting him to go to Saint Bernard rescue for a while now, and that I went through all sorts of plans to do so because my daddy needed some convincing.

Kathleen puts her arm around my shoulder and gives me a tender pat. "I see. You are doing the right thing for him. I'll make the arrangements for him through the rescue group," she says. "But first I need your permission to take him." She goes over to her desk and gets out a form, clipboard, and a pen. "What's his name?" Kathleen asks.

Mama says, "Killer."

But I say, "No, it's Beauregard," and that is what Kathleen writes down. After a few more questions Mama signs the bottom of the form to turn him over to the shelter.

I get this weird feeling in the pit of my stomach when I tell Beauregard good-bye. I want to give him a hug before Kathleen puts him in his cage, but for some reason I can't quite bring myself to. So I hold out my hand and say, "Shake." He automatically brings his paw up, and I grab it. "It was good knowing you, Beauregard," I say.

I think I hear him whimpering when we leave the room, but it's hard to tell because the other dogs in the room are barking. I don't look back.

Within a week Beauregard is gone. The rescue people came to pick him up on January 3. I know because Kathleen called to let me know. He was headed to a temporary foster home in Ohio.

Since we dropped him off at the shelter, the hardest part for me has been getting used to sleeping in my actual bed and not having Beauregard at my side. I keep on hanging my arm toward the floor, like I used to on the couch, but there is no collar to grasp, no soft dog hair working its way between my fingers.

Chapter 37

By the beginning of May hot weather has once again arrived in Greater Oaks. I flap the neckline of my T-shirt to create a slight breeze as I walk home from school.

I walk into the front yard, thinking how I should be feeling happy because I don't have to take care of Beauregard like before—no sploshed water on my sneakers, no steaming piles of poop to scoop, no bugs to shoo away while I spend time paying attention to him. I can just go inside and down a can of grape soda. But I still worry about that dog sometimes even though he's not here. I don't know what has happened to him; not all families post their adoption stories on the rescue site. So I do my best not to think about him, though he somehow creeps into my thoughts, like now.

As soon as I get in the front door, Justin Lee runs up to me. "Char-watt! Char-watt!" His pronunciation has gotten better. I'm no longer Char Char, which I had kind of gotten used to and thought was cute.

Justin Lee holds up his hand. "High fife," he says.

I reach out to give his hand a swat, but he jerks it away at the last moment and starts laughing his head off. Daddy taught him that trick, the fake out. They share the same sense of humor already.

Mama shakes her head and smiles. She doesn't seem a bit tired-looking anymore even though she should be. There's no problem with Justin Lee sleeping anymore, but he is into *everything*. Climbing, throwing, exploring, all at full speed ahead.

Now he's making a beeline for the stairs. Mama has a baby gate up, but he can climb over it, so she dashes over and grabs him.

"How about a snack, big boy?" she asks.

"Snack!" He nods.

"Charlotte, Kathleen from the animal shelter stopped by. She dropped something off for you. It's on the coffee table," Mama says, before disappearing into the kitchen with Justin Lee secured on her hip.

It's a letter. When I open it up, a picture flutters to the ground. I pick the picture up, and there is Beauregard with what I assume is his new family. Behind him a man and woman stand, both grinning. Identical twin girls, about my age, are kneeling on either side, hugging him. I quickly read the letter.

Dear Charlotte,

The Saint Bernard Rescue Foundation told us how Beauregard came up for adoption, and they said they would see that you got this letter.

Thank you for giving up such a wonderful dog so he'd have a better chance at life. We are so grateful! Beauregard is a member of our family now, and we can't imagine life without him. He goes everywhere with us, and people are always commenting on how gentle, calm, and affectionate he is. Not long ago both our daughters came down with the flu at the same time, and he played nursemaid for days, patiently lying between their beds, waiting for them to get better so they could once again play with him and rub his tummy (a favorite pastime of his!). We took him to obedience school soon after getting him. Sit, down, and stay were mastered quickly (and he already knew how to shake!), so now he is taking an advanced class. He enjoys being around the other dogs and also the treats used to reward him. He is so funny when we give him a dog treat; he just stares longingly at it, and then, when we give him the "take" command, you'd think he was at a tea party, he is so dainty and polite. I know it must have been difficult letting him go, but it is our hope this letter will reassure you: Beauregard is such a happy and content dog here with us. Thank you again from the bottom of our hearts.

The Windfields,

Joseph, Holly, Mindy, and Mandy

❀ ❀ ❀

I study the picture again. I can tell it was taken in a kitchen. The walls are painted a soft yellow. In the bottom corner of the photo I see plaid, a doggy bed. And I'm sure, even though I can't see it, somewhere in the room are food and water bowls printed with his name, just like in my dream.

I can't tell who is happier, Beauregard or those twin girls hugging him. Beauregard's nose is upturned, and I swear all that loose skin hanging from his mouth is gathered into a sloppy smile. The twins are hugging him so hard their inside cheeks are buried in the fur of his neck. I look at both their beaming faces, and something unexpected happens. I start to cry. Hard.

Justin Lee, done with his snack in the kitchen, comes running back to the living room. I quickly choke back my wayward sobs and wipe at my eyes. I fold the letter up and stick it and the picture back in the envelope, placing it on the coffee table.

"High fife," Justin Lee says, holding up his hand. I go to smack his hand, fully expecting him to

221

jerk it away, but he doesn't, and my hand splats onto something slimy.

"Yuck!" I quickly withdraw my hand and look at it as Justin Lee falls, laughing, to the floor.

Though disgusted, I laugh, too.

Mama hurries into the room, a damp washcloth in her hand. "Sorry. Banana," she tells me, grabbing Justin Lee to clean off the squished banana remaining on his hand.

"Oh." I head to the bathroom to wash my own hand off.

After I'm done washing off my hand, I give Mama a break by reading a story to Justin Lee. Reading to him is about the only thing that will keep him still. He snuggles into my lap and grins up at me, tiny baby teeth visible.

When I close the book, I hear the back door and voices.

"Look at what Daddy brought home!" I hear Agnes say.

I hear Mama in the kitchen yell, "What on *earth*?"

I rush into the kitchen with Justin Lee still in my arms.

Daddy has a golf bag with clubs slung over his shoulder.

"You don't play golf," Mama says.

"Not yet. Hank, the accountant at work, got a new set and practically gave these to me. Worth about six hundred dollars. I only paid seventy-five."

"We can't afford the green fees," Mama says.

"Hank is a member of West Townfield Country Club. He has five times he can bring a guest for free. He said he can bring me along when he goes, just so I can try it out." Daddy sets down the clubs, spreads his legs apart, and takes an imaginary swing.

"Okay, Arnold Palmer." Mama laughs.

The whole family is in the kitchen and grinning and things feel the way they should be.

No dog worries.

No Mama worries.

Back to normal.

Finally.

Chapter 38

The following day is Friday, and after school Luanne, Grace, and I walk to Petunia's. She recovered well enough to come back home in March, although Rhonda, Barth, and Amber Rose moved in with her because she needed extra care. Rhonda said it was an adjustment at first for them all but that Petunia truly enjoys the baby and that it all seems to have worked out.

When we reach the house, the three of us stand in front for a moment, gaping with admiration at the new paint job we see. Last week Rhonda took the snapshot of Petunia's father after he had finished painting the house to a paint store. The shop used the photo to mix up some new paint to match. So now the house looks just as cheerful and happy on the outside as it does on the inside.

We finally go up to the porch to ring the doorbell and after a few moments see Petunia's face as the door opens.

"The house looks great!" Luanne says.

"Oh, thanks," Petunia says. "I was so afraid they wouldn't get the color right. But it ended up being just perfect. My father would approve, I'm sure." Petunia showers us with her half grin, and it conveys just as much joy as any full grin would have.

Rhonda is at the beauty shop, Barth is at work, and Amber Rose is at her grandma's house, so it's just the four of us. On the way to the kitchen table I walk by my gift to Petunia. My work of art is hanging on a wall in the parlor. It looks grand, if I do say so myself. I'm hoping the new painting I started last night of Beauregard and his new family will turn out just as good.

We get settled at the kitchen table. As Grace deals

the cards, I open my backpack and take out the letter and picture of Beauregard's new family. I brought them along to share with everyone since they all played a part in his newfound happiness.

"The girls look really nice," Grace says.

"And the parents, too!" says Luanne.

"Oh, how wonderful," Petunia says after she is done reading the letter and looking at the picture. "Beauregard is positively glowing. What an amazing thing to have happened to him and that family. A happy ending. That's what we all want, isn't it?"

I nod, unable to speak because I start to get all choked up again. I feel hot and red-faced. Just when I think I'm about to burst out bawling, Luanne says, "Charlotte, I just passed. You need to decide which suit to call trump."

I study my hand. I have an ace of hearts, a queen of hearts, and a jack of diamonds. "Hearts," I say, relieved at having successfully shoved the teary feeling away.

I'm not sad, and everything is fine and dandy, so why on earth do I keep on feeling like I need to cry?

226

❀ ❀ ❀

After Petunia's, we walk to the shelter over on Fenton Street. I want to thank Kathleen for bringing over the letter from Beauregard's new family and for all her help.

When we troop through the door, Kathleen looks up from the front desk and greets us with a "Hey, girls!" She stands up. "Did you get the letter?" she asks me.

"Yes. Thanks. I feel so much better now, knowing where he is."

"Couldn't ask for him to have a better home," Kathleen says.

"I really appreciate what you did, making the arrangements with the rescue group and everything. I bet Beauregard appreciates it, too."

"Well, that's what we're here for. You all want to visit some of the dogs we have?" she asks. "They'd love the attention if you have some time to spare." Without waiting for an answer, she starts walking. We follow her back to the dog adoption room. Five dogs welcome us with their tails wagging.

"You know, I was thinking of trying to start a volunteer program for kids to come for a couple of hours a week to walk the dogs. Maybe brush them or bathe them and spend time with them, too. Would you three be interested? As long as your parents give permission, of course."

Luanne and Grace give an enthusiastic "yes!"

I don't say anything. One of the dogs reminds me a bit of Beauregard. Large, boxy head, a bit of drool hanging out of his mouth, but with a smooth solid reddish coat. A mixed breed of some sort. He looks at me with deep brown eyes and whimpers. I flash back to when I last saw Beauregard, right here at the shelter, and I suddenly wish with all my heart I had hugged him after all. I feel my throat tighten up.

"Sure, I'll volunteer," I tell Kathleen, my voice kind of high and squeaky-sounding.

Oh, why did I just say that? After all I went through to get rid of Beauregard, and here I'll be doing dog chores again. Am I crazy?

I blink away a few tears and stick my hand through the cage to pet the dog. And, like a ton of bricks, it hits me why I've been so emotional lately. I miss Beauregard. A bunch.

Maybe I *am* a dog person?

Even though I wasn't exactly born one, I happen to feel like one now.

"What's his name?" I ask Kathleen.

"The people who turned him in called him Fang."

I lean in and whisper to him, "We'll have to do something about that name of yours."

He thumps his tail. I find myself wondering if I bring some gingersnaps with me when I come back, how long it will take me to teach this dog to shake hands.

I guess I might as well admit this straight up.

I can hardly wait to find out.

Afterword

I had a Saint Bernard growing up. We got her when she was a few months old and named her Heidi. Shortly after she arrived, I came down with the mumps, and Heidi stayed snuggled up on the couch with me for days. She made having the mumps easy, almost enjoyable. I loved having her company, and she loved being with me. Heidi grew into 150 pounds of pure sweetness and affection. She was an integral and important part of our family. We truly doted on that big, slobbery dog of ours.

Charlotte and Beauregard's story came into being nearly thirty-six years after my bout with the mumps.

I was on my way to pick up my son at the home of his friend who lived an hour and a half away. During the long drive there, I noticed a sad looking Saint Bernard chained up in someone's backyard. I began to worry about that dog, even though I honestly didn't know the particulars of his situation. It could have been that he was just waiting for his owner to come home, bring him inside, and lavish attention on him. But I also knew that perhaps this might be all his life amounted to—loneliness bound to a chain. I thought about that dog long after I drove by him, and the echoes became *The Dog Days of Charlotte Hayes.*

While researching this story I learned about the Saint Bernard Rescue Foundation. You can visit them at www.saintrescue.org, just like Charlotte did. Each year they place hundreds of these big, wonderful dogs into loving homes. There are also breed rescue groups for nearly every sort of dog imaginable—from the enormous Irish wolfhound to the tiny Chihuahua and all sizes in between. These groups are dedicated to making sure the dogs in their care have the best life possible ahead of them. And, of course, there are millions of mixed breeds in shelters across the nation, eagerly waiting for families to call their own. Like Beauregard, they all deserve a happy ending.